A
HEART
TO THE
HAWKS

A
HEART
TO THE
HAWKS

DON MOSER

Atheneum   New York
1975

A Margaret K. McElderry Book

Copyright © 1975 by Don Moser
All rights reserved
Published simultaneously in Canada
by McClelland & Stewart, Ltd.
Manufactured in the United States of America
by Halliday Lithograph Corporation
West Hanover, Massachusetts
Designed by Suzanne Haldane
First Edition

Library of Congress Cataloging in Publication Data

Moser, Don.   A heart to the hawks.
"A Margaret K. McElderry book."
SUMMARY: Fourteen-year-old Mike's passion for
natural history causes him to fight a land-developer's
destruction of his woodland haven first with
persuasion and then with violence.
[1. Conservation of natural resources—Fiction.
2. Ohio—Fiction] I. Title.   PZ7.M84694H4   [Fic]
74-18190   ISBN 0-689-50024-6

For Mark, Gil, and Dennis

A
HEART
TO THE
HAWKS

On an afternoon in early summer Mike Harrington was reading *African Game Trails* by Theodore Roosevelt for the second time, enjoying the book as much as he had last spring, and committing short passages to memory as he read along.

Though he was lying on the grass behind a big log at the edge of the pond, he could feel the equatorial sun beat heavy on his head, see the great herds shimmering in the distant mirage and vultures wheeling slowly in the hot, white sky. Cuninghame and Tarlton, the white hunters, were there with him, and brave young Kermit Roosevelt, and of course the ex-president himself, T.R. After reading about the incident of the wounded lion, Mike closed the book, shifted slightly in the grass, raised his eyes slowly above the top of the log that concealed him. Carefully he scanned from left to right over the glassy black surface of the water beyond the log, his eyes pausing now and again, acutely sensitive to each movement, even the stir of a leaf. After a long moment he rose, quietly moved out from behind the log and into the slick dark water. He felt the handle of his insect net smooth against his palm, the dark water pressing his boots against his legs like strong hands. He moved cautiously, his feet sinking into the muck, the water rising to his knees, then to his thighs. The smell of rotting vegetation was strong in his nostrils, the sun hot on his back. It was a long time before he saw his quarry. He froze, became a stone figure in the black water. Only his eyes moved as he watched, judging its distance, its rate of movement. *"Dytiscus."* He said the word aloud but so softly that it was scarcely audible to his own sensitive ears. He shifted the net slightly in his hand. Its familiar touch steadied him. He stood absolutely still. He held his breath. Then, cat-quick, he thrust forward.

He came up, a fraction of a second later, with the three-inch-long larva of a common water beetle in the bag of his insect net. He peered down into the net and examined it —segmented, voracious, sickle-jawed—a water tiger, it was called. "Holy cow!" he breathed. As he stood there, excited and pleased, he heard, from far back in the woods and old farm fields to the south of the pond, an unfamiliar sound. He listened for a moment. It was a kind of guttural roar, but so softened by distance that it seemed no more than a hoarse whisper, with an overlay of sharper sound, like the clanking of armor of a far-off battalion. "Rhino, probably." He shrugged. *"Diceros bicornis."*

4

It was in early June, 1946, in the summer of his four-teenth year, that Michael Harrington thus first sensed the presence of the bulldozer.

For someone who intended to be a polar explorer, fal-coner, first conqueror of Everest, oceanographer, Eagle Scout, field herpetologist, big-game hunter (for scientific purposes only), and frequent contributor of articles to the *National Geographic Magazine*, as well as the world's greatest living authority on freshwater biology, it wasn't a bad place to grow up. His home, in a suburb east of Cleveland, Ohio, was surrounded on three sides by de-fense plants, just converted back from the manufacture of tanks and airplane engines to the making of automobiles and refrigerators and the other truck of civilian life; and by streets of orderly, close-set houses with small yards in front and back. But on the fourth side were woodlands and old farms, many of them abandoned and gone back to second-growth timber, and a net of dirt and gravel roads that stretched away into the rural counties beyond. It was a wedge of country driven into the heart of a city or, to say it better, a city hammered down over a last re-maining spike of country, its development halted by years of war and the shortage of construction materials. On a summer night, if he looked north from the house, Mike saw the lamps of progress; if he looked south, he saw rac-coons.

The house he grew up in, and a few acres of the land surrounding it, had been bought a dozen years before by Mike's father, in one of his characteristic moments of ex-cess. Once the main house of a great farmstead, the white frame building was a century and a half old, and had been frequently added to and perhaps even subtracted from

5

over the decades; from the front, with its broad span of white-columned porch, it looked like the mansion of a Carolina plantation; from behind, it resembled a chicken coop. The house had four entrances, three stairways, two living rooms, two kitchens, and one bathroom. It had leaded-glass windows in the living room and enough book-cases to accommodate the Cleveland Public Library. In the kitchen it had a five-foot-tall, ornately wrought heating stove named Frankenstein, a mass of iron angels, curl-icues, and isinglass windows; the stove ate anthracite egg coal like peanuts, glowed cherry-red and, when in full bloom, couldn't be stood within ten feet of. In the hall closet there were—never discarded more through general disorganization than sentiment—six of his grandfather's straw boaters, the annual donning of which had always been, in that house, the first sign of spring. There were—leaving out for now Mike's own collections—termites in the floors, bats in the chimneys, rats in the cellar, and rac-coons in the garbage can. In the winter the furnace heated the front of the house, Frankenstein heated the back, and the upstairs was heated by nothing except—during the years of her reign—his grandmother's exple-tives when she found her false teeth frozen in the water glass after a coolish night. The stairs creaked, the floor groaned, the roof leaked, the chimneys smoked, and the pipes thundered as if connected to the earth's molten core. The house was full of nooks, crannies, *cul-de-sacs*, closets, cupboards, and built-in chests of drawers large enough for the disposal of bodies, and in his younger days when Mike had played commandos with his little brother Andy, the game frequently had to be called at dinnertime with neither side having made contact with the enemy.

In the way of outbuildings, the house had a woodshed, which belonged to Mike for his collections, the barn, which belonged to his father for the tractor, and the garage, which belonged to the Cadillac. The Cadillac, a 1935 limousine with the glass partition removed, was so long that the back end stuck out the garage door, the front bumper thus remaining bright chrome while the back one disappeared beneath a coating of rust.

During its heyday the house had been inhabited by eight human beings: Mike and his brother, his mother and father, his paternal grandfather and grandmother, and his aunt and uncle. The two old people had died, one shortly after the other, in the last year of the war, and not long after V-J day, the housing shortage having eased slightly, his aunt and uncle had moved to a city apartment of their own, leaving the rest of them rattling through the rooms like marbles in a can, sometimes spending hours and even days without encountering each other except at meals, and on the way to the bathroom.

Around the house lay a lush ruin of flowers and ornamental plants, all untrimmed, uncultivated, and uncared for, but growing with a feral vitality that was almost frightening; Mike could gouge tracks through a narcissus bed in the afternoon, and next morning find the signs of his passage obliterated by a rush of new blossoms. The lilacs bordering the brick drive grew not on bushes but great shaggy trees. Roses erupted from the tear-shaped carriage circle, beds of monster irises bordered the house, vast banks of daffodils and jonquils lined the long reaches of the yard, unkempt forsythia and orange-blossom hedges littered an acre with their petals.

Fanning out to the south, toward the rise of Portage

Escarpment, lay the network of old farm fields and orchards and pastures of the original farmstead. Beyond the Escarpment other farms stretched away, many of them fallow since the depression, some fallow for decades—a terrain inhabited by possums and foxes, by crumbling barns, and sagging houses with the windows long since broken out and rain-stained wallpaper curling down in strips. All of these lands lay beyond the boundaries of Mr. Harrington's mortgage, but there were few fences in those days, and what few there were had fallen down. There were neither signs of ownership nor signs that said keep out; hoboes jungled up there sometimes but not often, since it was so far from the railroad tracks; neckers went there occasionally, but usually preferred the more manicured environs of Sandy Creek Park off to the southeast. The logic of geography and history, if not the law, annexed the lands to the Harringtons', and Mike had squatter's rights.

There were two ways to get from the pond, a quarter of a mile back from the rim of the Escarpment, to the house. The shortest and easiest way was along a well-trodden path down a shallow gulley to the east. On the second route, to the west, there was no path except the track that Mike had bushwhacked out during the spring: it emerged from the woods behind the little house of Mr. Miklos Karman, the Harringtons' only near neighbor on the south side of the avenue. More and more these days, Mike took the second route down from the pond, on the off chance that he might run into Angeline. He started off that way on this afternoon, his collecting net over one shoulder, and hanging from the other a war-surplus gas-mask bag containing his instruments, his copy of *African Game Trails*, and the pint Mason jar that held his prize, the water tiger. Leaving the pond, he stopped for a moment to look pridefully at his trees. They were three enormous white oaks, each as thick through the butt as he stood tall and with branches the size of a large man's waist; their foliage was so dense as to shade out anything trying to grow beneath, so that they created a kind of open, parklike room, its roof supported by the three columns of their trunks. Each now bore a small metal plaque, the result of Mike's work early in the year, when he had measured each tree with a piece of twine, calculated its height using the shadow technique, and photographed each one with his father's Kodak. After he submitted his data, a man came to examine the trees, and a couple of weeks later the plaques arrived in the mail: he had just nailed them to the trunks a few days before, and he still stopped to read them each time he left the pond. Each plaque read:

WHITE OAK
(*Quercus alba*)

This is a Moses Cleaveland Tree. It was standing here as part of the original forest when Moses Cleaveland landed at the mouth of the Cuyahoga River, July 22nd, 1796. Let us preserve it as a living memorial to the first settlers of the Western Reserve.
—THE SESQUICENTENNIAL COMMISSION

Mike walked to each of the three trees in turn, read each of the identical plaques. Then, feeling quite pleased with himself, he started back down through the woods.

A little later, he came out of the trees behind Karman's chicken coop, where the little flock of white leghorns squawked and scratched the dirt behind their wire enclosure, then walked along the rows of beans, squash, tomatoes, and corn, all orderly and neatly tended and so unlike the results of his own father's overweening attempt at agriculture. Although Mr. Karman's real job was as a lineman for the telephone company, when it came to farming, he obviously knew what he was doing. Mr. Karman was a brown-skinned, hump-backed little man, fifteen years out of Hungary, who moved with the arm-swinging lope of an orangutan and spoke, on the rare occasions when he did, in halting and broken English. In the evenings and on weekends he worked in his garden or around his chicken house, humping over a spade or hoe until it was too dark to see. Or else he went off in the woods to plunder whatever was in season—mushrooms, blackberries, walnuts, even mistletoe that he gathered with the aid of his lineman's climbers. He knew the woods better than anyone except Mike himself, but didn't seem to care about, or even see, anything he couldn't eat or sell down at the Farmer's Market.

As Mike walked along through the field, he saw Angeline sitting on the back steps of the little house. He walked more slowly, carrying the net over his shoulder with the handle under the crook of his elbow, as Boone would have carried his long rifle. He checked to make sure that his shirt collar was turned up in back.

As he approached, she looked up from the magazine she had been reading. "Hi," she said, a little startled.

"Hi, Angeline," he said, and stopped in front of her and tried to think of something else to say. He never understood how she could be so beautiful, given the general ugliness of the rest of her family. If her father's nose was like a beak, hers was small and neat. Her skin was very white against the dark long hair. She had conical breasts and legs so smooth they might have been sculpted from ivory. She wore a dark skirt and a white blouse and bobby socks so white that she must have bleached them for hours, and her loafers glinted from polishing. "Are you enjoying your vacation?" he asked.

"It's all right," she said. "I bet you miss school, though, since you're so smart."

Mike felt himself flushing. "Oh, I don't miss it," he said. "Now school's out I get time to work on my collections." He stood there, looking down at the pennies in her loafers. They were bright copper pennies that looked as if they had been newly minted.

His hip boots, he saw, were covered with mud.

"Well," he said, "well, I guess I'd better get going, Angeline."

"You want a Kool-Aid?" she asked.

"Oh," he said. "Well, yes, it got pretty hot collecting, you know."

"Some's made. I'll go in and get it."

Waiting for her, he sat down on the steps, picked up her magazine, *Photoplay*. On the cover was a picture of Jeanne Crane holding a dog and a headline that said, "Romantic report from June Allyson." He flipped through the pages. It's like this to be Mrs. Gregory Peck. If you were the ranch guest of Betty Grable. With courage she found her break with Orson Welles; to dance time Rita Hayworth has regained her gaiety with Tony Martin. Ad for a new Tarzan movie, with Brenda Joyce wearing a leopard-skin sarong and high-heeled ankle-strap shoes.

Way they always dress in the bush, isn't it? Mike said

11

to himself. I wonder why she reads this junk? I wonder if I should give her Osa Johnson's *I Married Adventure*? A girl, he supposed, might like that.

He flipped on through the pages to a spot that Angeline had marked with a flower from her mother's garden. "My Washington Diary," by Elizabeth Taylor. His eye ran down the page. "I wanted to wear my black velvet, my grown-upiest one. Mummie wanted me to wear my black velvet Tyrolean outfit with the white long-sleeved blouse. Daddy wanted me to wear my red velvet suit. And Howard liked my pale blue cashmere dress with the crystal beads."

"Oh, for crying out loud," Mike said.

Angeline came out a few minutes later with two glasses of Kool-Aid, grape, and sat down on the step beside him. He drank a bit, said, "That's very nice of you, Angeline."

"You looked so hot," she said. She looked not at him but straight ahead. In profile, he thought, she actually did look a little like Elizabeth Taylor. She smelled good. How can she always be so *clean*? he wondered.

"I was reading about Elizabeth Taylor going to Washington," Angeline said. "Do you know, she went there to help with the March of Dimes and visited all the crippled children. And she is just the same age as me, our birthdays are just two weeks apart."

"Really?"

"Mike, you read so much, do you know what a dryad is?"

"A dryad. Kind of a fairy, I guess, that lives in the woods. There aren't any, really."

"Oh. Maxine Arnold says that Elizabeth Taylor resembles a dryad," Angeline picked up the magazine, studied the picture with the story. "She does look sort of like a lovely fairy, don't you think? Do you know they told her that she was too little to play in *National Velvet* and so she prayed, and she grew three inches in three months, and she got the part."

"Wow!" Mike said.

"Did you see *National Velvet*?"

"I don't go to the movies much, Angeline."

"I've seen it five times, and now Daddy won't let me go anymore. I saw her in *Lassie Come Home* three times. I thought Roddy McDowell was truly wonderful too."

"I read that," Mike said. "When I was a kid I used to read all those dog books by Eric Knight and Albert Payson Terhune."

"Do you know what? One morning I saw you coming up through the field with your dog, and it made me think of the movie—I thought you looked just like Roddy McDowell and Lassie."

"Really?" Mike felt himself flushing. "Well," he said. "Well. That's bully."

"What?" she asked.

"Bully. Theodore Roosevelt used to say that."

"Oh," she said. "I didn't know about that."

"I've read an awful lot about Theodore Roosevelt. And his son Kermit. I think Theodore Roosevelt was our greatest president."

"He was my father's favorite, too," Angeline said primly. "My father cried when he died."

"Your father cried when he died?"

"Yes," Angeline said. "My mother did too. They don't like President Truman."

"Truman?" Mike said. "Oh—oh, yeah, I see. But that was"—he stopped himself abruptly.

"What?" Angeline asked.

13

"Never mind," Mike said. Is it possible, he wondered, to love someone who doesn't know Theodore Roosevelt from Franklin Roosevelt? He watched Angeline sip her Kool-Aid, lick a drop from her lips with a tongue small and neat as a cat's. Yes, he decided.

They sat in silence for a while. Mike tried to decide whether to show Angeline his *Dytiscus* larva, finally concluding that he had better not. Suddenly there was an eruption of meaningless Hungarian from the direction of the little chicken coop across the garden. A moment later Mr. Karman emerged from behind the wire fencing and began walking through the rows of squash toward the house. He had a mash bucket in one hand and a spade in the other. At every other step he lifted the spade into the air and slammed it against the ground so hard that little spurts of dust flew into the air. He came across the garden metronomically slamming the spade and occasionally bursting out with some unintelligible expletive. "Daddy sure looks mad," Angeline said.

"Oh, boy," Mike said. "I got a feeling . . ."

The man reached the house and stopped there and stared at them, the spade clutched in his fist. He glared at Mike from behind his beaky nose. Mike stood up quickly. So did Angeline.

"One more today," the man said. "Now, five."

"I'm sure it wasn't the redtails," Mike began.

"Five," the man said.

"According to John Bichard May's *Hawks of North America*, the redtail, *Buteo Jamaicensis*, almost never . . ."

"Five."

". . . eats domestic fowl but subsists largely on a diet of rodents and . . ."

14

"Five," Mr. Karman thundered, and slammed the spade on the ground. "Every day work. Dig, plant, haul. And. And what? The raccoon eat the tomato. The possum eat the corn. The bird eat the seed. Now the hawk eat the chicken. Five chicken now in two week. In old country not like this."

"But," Mike said.

"I get gun," Karman said. He stabbed the spade into the soft earth of his wife's flower bed, stomped up the steps and into the house.

Angeline shook her head and looked at Mike sympathetically. "Sometimes Daddy can be *utterly* unreasonable," she said.

Mike's room on the second floor of the old house was large and cluttered. Along one wall was a row of battered old tables, a couple of them salvaged from the barn, and a workbench his grandfather had built for him. They were heaped with bottles of formalin, cigar boxes full of pinned insects, a collection of carefully blown birds' eggs nesting on cotton, spreading boards on which butterflies were drying, and a row of small screen cages, battery jars, and cheap aquaria. They were filled with aquatic insects, newts, half a dozen varieties of frogs. In one aquarium was an enormous toad named the Nilghai after the corpulent journalist in Kipling's *The Light that Failed*. In another were a pair of finger-length pickerel with long vicious jaws, in still another a pair of beautiful green and silver baby bass. There were no snakes, lizards, or turtles in the room now—his mother had banished that part of his collection to the woodshed earlier in the year when his milk snake had escaped and she had found it coiled neatly in the middle of her bed. On the walls of the room

15

he'd tacked a picture of a peregrine falcon he'd cut from a magazine, and a collection of signs and nameplates he and his friend John Corcoran had pried off gas pumps, electric fans, and movie seats. Next to his bed was a stack of library books—the school librarian had given him permission to take out six at a time instead of the normal quota of three. The room was messy—his mother refused to enter it as long as he kept his collections there, and so he had to keep it clean himself, which he was lax about, particularly during the summer when there was so much to do.

Mike sat at the workbench staring into a battery jar where the big water tiger now hung head downward from a sprig of elodea, its great curved jaws waiting for anything that might come by. "Hannibal," Mike said.

"What?" said a voice from behind him. He turned and saw that his little brother Andy had come into the room.

"I'm going to name him Hannibal."

"What's that?" Andy asked.

"He was a great Carthaginian general," Mike said. "He crossed the Alps with elephants 2,000 years ago."

"It sure is nice to have a brother who knows everything," Andy said wryly.

"It sure is nice to have a little brother who's a wise guy," Mike said. He looked around. Andy had the top off a bottle of formalin and was sniffing at it. Andy was ten and since he'd been able to walk had spent much of his time smelling things. His mother said that if you cut off that boy's nose he couldn't find his way from one room to the other. "Whee-ew," Andy said, his nose wrinkling.

"How about keeping your nose out of my specimens," Mike said. "Sometime this summer I'm going to get a cyanide killing jar from Ward's scientific supply house, and the first time you start sniffing around that, you're going to drop dead twice."

Andy screwed the top back on the jar. "You're going camping tonight. I heard you talking to Corcoran on the phone."

"So what?"

"So how about letting me come?"

"That's a preposterous idea," Mike said. "All we need is you stumbling around while we're collecting. Besides, Mom wouldn't let you come."

"She would if you said you'd look out for me."

"Campers have to look out for themselves."

"Oh, nuts to you," Andy said.

"Amscray," Mike said.

Andy sighed. "My brother the nut."

Mike looked up at his brother.

"Oh, all right, I'm going," Andy said. He turned around and started out the door and almost ran into his father coming in. "Hi, Dad," Andy said.

"Hello, son." The man stopped inside the doorway, looked around.

"Einstein's got some new weird bug," Andy said dryly. "As usual. Ugh. Can I stay up for 'Hermit's Cave' tonight?"

"I suppose so," his father said.

"Hubba hubba," Andy said, and launched out the door, suddenly as a cork popped from a gun.

"Mind if I sit down, Mike?" the man said.

"No, go ahead. I was just looking at a new specimen."

His father sat down on the bed, put his hands on his knees, looked around the room. He was an inventor of

17

sorts. A large shambling man, he worked for the Atlas Tractor Corporation, not on the tractors and bulldozers themselves but on pipelines and conveyors and overhead cranes and other production-line machinery. Because he lacked formal education, he was not qualified to be an engineer and worked merely as a draftsman, an artisan with T squares, french curves, protractors, and number six pencils with points so long, sharp, and hard they could have been used as darts. On his job he was unable to do more than render the work of others, but in his spare time he created designs for devices made of steel, pipe, and gears, most of them having to do with industrial processes and therefore incomprehensible to Mike. He had always believed that one of his inventions would make him rich, but they never had, either because they failed, or because their patents became the property of the long succession of companies he had worked for.

With his sharp pencils, his drawing paper, and slide rule he had a genius for mechanical design. Yet what he loved was the machines themselves. His passion was the touch of tool steel and the feel of grease and oil, the smooth slide of pistons and the silky meshing of gears. When he saw a machine, he wanted to fondle it. But he was probably the worst mechanic since the invention of the wheel. His old Cadillac and his antique Fordson tractor were his life's romances. He spent his Sundays flailing at their venerable innards, trying to keep them in something approximating running condition. His encounters with his machines were disastrous. He twisted the heads off bolts, stripped threads, mashed his knuckles till his hands were all blood and grease, and—for all his mechanical sensitivity at the drawing board—when he put something back together, he usually wound up with a piece or two left over. The Cadillac wheezed, knocked, and backfired like a flatulent rhinoceros; the Fordson whistled through its leaking headgasket like a wild canary. He was a man who wanted to play a concerto—but his only talent was to compose it.

He sat now on the bed, observing the room. He sniffed the air. "This place smells," he said. "Smells like a morgue. What's that thing?" He nodded at the battery jar in front of Mike.

"A water tiger. The larva of *Dytiscus*."

"Oh," the man said. "I suppose it's cannibalistic or something."

"It eats tadpoles, usually."

The man shuddered. "Don't you ever get anything that doesn't eat something else?" he asked.

"Everything eats something, Dad."

Mr. Harrington sighed. "Some fathers have sons who keep white rabbits," he said, "and all they eat is lettuce. Some fathers have sons who keep dogs, and all they eat is Ken'l Ration, and they learn to roll over and shake hands. My son keeps something called a water tiger that probably eats small children when it can get them."

"Oh, come on." Mike laughed.

"Are you going up to that pond again tonight?"

"Corcoran and I are camping out."

"You know your mother really worries about you when you do that."

"There really isn't anything to worry about," Mike said. "There aren't any lions and tigers, you know."

The man stood up. "All right," he said. "I want to show you something in the kitchen before you go. You can see

19

it when you stop to steal all the food out of the cupboard."

Later, Mike clumped downstairs in his hipboots, carrying his net and a rucksack stuffed with an army-surplus jungle hammock and a wool sleeping bag that was never warm enough, even in summer. His father was at the oilcloth-covered table in the larger of the two kitchens, with his drawing board set up in front of him. He had a long strip of smooth metal in his hands, and he was bending it and flexing it as Andy watched, bug-eyed. Mike set his gear down. "What's that thing?" he asked.

"That's what's going to make us all rich." His mother's voice came from the other kitchen.

"All right, Martha," his father said.

"Is it a new invention?" Mike asked.

"It's a Draft-eez, dummy," Andy said, looking pleased with himself.

The man bent the steel strip into a full circle, released one end, and it snapped back into shape again. "Come here and take a look. I'll explain how this works." He took a soft pencil, doodled on the drawing paper in front of him. Then he slid his T square up and down the board a few times. "See how my drawing gets smudged when I run my T square over it? That's the bane of a draftsman's life. The more you work on a drawing, the more you mess it up with the T square sliding over it. Then you have to keep cleaning it up with an eraser. Now, watch." He removed the T square from the board, pinned his metal strip down one side, pinned a duplicate metal strip on the other side, replaced the T square. Then he ran the T square back and forth over the drawing again. "See," he said, "it's spring steel, with a little arch to it. The T square runs along like

20

on tracks, without touching the paper. Now, when you want to draw, you press down on the square, and flatten the arch in the spring steel, and draw your line. When you're finished, you just release the pressure." He slipped his fingers off the T square, and it popped an inch into the air.

"Well," the man said, "I don't really have them perfected yet. I need a lighter gauge steel or maybe a flatter arch, but I'll work that out." He grinned at Mike. "I call them Draft-eez," he said. "I've already sent myself a registered letter, and I'm going to make a patent application."

"And then we're all going to get rich." Mrs. Harrington's voice drifted from the other room. "And move to Shaker Heights and eat porterhouse steak three times a day."

"That's terrific, Dad," Mike said.

"Do you know how many draftsmen there are in the United States?" his father asked.

"No."

"I don't know exactly, but there are thousands and thousands. Do you know how many schools teach mechanical drawing? Every high school in the country. Ten or fifteen or twenty or twenty-five drawing boards in every high school in these United States. Think about that for a minute."

"It's a bully idea, Dad," Mike said.

"A *bully* idea?" Andy said.

"Oh, pipe down," Mike said.

His mother emerged from the other kitchen, stood looking at him. "Are you going to have supper?" she asked. She was a small woman, dark-haired and Irish, alternately feisty and sentimental, with a large capacity to either fight or cry as the spirit moved her. Her surface was prickly and cross, her interior easily touched. She pinched pennies, despised dirt, hated sloth, believed in hard common sense, and went to pieces in sad movies. "Are you going to have supper?" she repeated.

"I'll eat up in the woods," Mike said. "We'll cook out."

She lifted her hands, palms upward. "Lord preserve us," she said. "A boy can stay home and have a good dinner, and instead he wants to go out in the woods and eat beans out of a can."

"I thought there might be some Dinty Moore's," Mike said.

"Some Dinty Moore's, he says." She turned back toward the kitchen. "Look for yourself, and you needn't ask me for any help." Her voice drifted back. "I will set the table if we can remove the world's greatest invention."

His father sighed, picked up his drawing board and went off toward the living room. Mike went out into the little kitchen and rooted around on the shelves till he found a can of Dinty Moore's beef stew and a can of Heinz pork and beans. He stuffed them into his pack, restrapped it, hoisted it to his shoulders, and started back out. His mother barred his way. "Just a minute," she said, and thrust a packet of waxed paper toward him. He took it, saw that it contained a couple of chunks of cold chicken. "Thanks," he said.

"Do you have your pajamas?" the woman asked.

"In my pack," he lied.

"Well, don't catch your death."

As Mike walked out, Andy, still at the table, brought his hand up to his eyebrow in a slow salute. "Have a *bully* time," he said.

22

John Corcoran, also known as Toad, lived in a small well-to-do neighborhood of tree-lined streets and carefully tended lawns, a residential thumb sticking south into the farmland from the city, and only about half a mile from Mike's pond. Corcoran had been Mike's best friend since primary school, the two of them drawn close by their shared passion for science. Corcoran's own sciences were chemistry and physics and electronics, and he could solve complicated arithmetical problems in his head, just about as well as Joel Kupperman of the Quiz Kids.

Like Mike, Corcoran read voraciously, and the two of them had been swapping books since the age of ten. They had started with *The Wind in the Willows,* which had got them to calling each other Toad and Mole, and they had never quite outgrown the habit, although they were a little embarrassed by the nicknames now and never used them within hearing of other people. Currently, their favorite book was Kipling's *The Light that Failed,* the story of a young war correspondent-artist who goes blind at the height of his powers and dies with his love for his beautiful childhood sweetheart still unrequited. It had moved them both to tears—though neither would admit that to the other—and both of them now could quote long passages of its dialogue by heart.

When Mike knocked on the back door of Corcoran's house, his friend opened it himself. He was Mike's age, although a little taller and heavier, and he wore his hair in a conservative duck's ass. His father, a moderately successful pharmaceuticals salesman, was liberal with money, and Corcoran dressed very sharp at school, with pegged pants and maroon shirts, but he was in his old chemical-stained jeans now.

"Mole." He grinned.

"Revolting Toad," said Mike. "I've been waiting for you over at Basecamp."

"Sorry. I had an experiment going. I'm almost finished, though. Come on down to the lab."

Corcoran's father, selling on the road so much of the time, made up for his absence by endowing his son with almost anything he asked for in the way of money for chemicals and equipment. As a result, the basement laboratory, while smaller than the chemistry lab at school, was at least as well equipped. One end of the basement glittered with racks of test tubes, beakers, retorts, and

Erlenmeyer flasks. Boxes and bottles of chemicals lined shelves that stretched to the ceiling; there was even a gas line for a pair of Bunsen burners. A chemical valence chart and a portrait of Albert Einstein were taped to the wall. At the other end of the basement was a long workbench littered with power tools, the innards of half a dozen old radios, spark coils out of Model-T Fords, dismembered electric motors, and magnets. Standing above the bench was a complex assemblage of wires, electric motors, generators, and condensers—Corcoran's latest perpetual-motion machine.

"I'm working on the nitrate ring test," Corcoran said, and held up a test tube of colorless liquid. "Qualitative analysis. I've only got two more to go."

Corcoran had spent most of the last year of general science class—since he knew all of the material being taught—trying to design a rubber-band-powered helicopter that would actually fly, constructing a Tesla coil with which he and Mike jammed every radio in Greater Cleveland, and building a series of perpetual-motion machines, the most perpetual of which remained in motion for twenty-one minutes. This summer, he had explained to Mike, his project was to complete his study of high school chemistry, so that on the first day of class he could ask Mr. Ray, the teacher, to give him the final exam. If he passed it with an *A,* which he would do easily, he would ask to be released during class periods to work on his own experiments.

"Now watch," he said to Mike. He held up a pipette. "This is how the nitrate ring test works. I've mixed my test solution with three cc's of ferrous sulfate—now I pipette in a few drops of sulphuric acid. Very carefully. At the interface we'll get a formation of $FeSO_4\text{-}NO$, and that will make a visible brown ring."

"You'll probably screw it up," Mike said.

"Toad the mad chemist never screws it up." Corcoran peeped into the tube.

"Reading anything?" Mike asked.

"The life of Steinmetz," Corcoran said, eyes glued to the tube. "The electronic wizard. He worked for General Electric, and he smoked big cigars. One day he came to work, and they'd put up a no-smoking sign in the lab. He went to his desk and started packing up. They said, 'What are you doing?' He said, 'I'm quitting, because the signs say no smoking.' They said, 'Oh, that doesn't mean you, Mr. Steinmetz.' He said, 'If nobody else smokes, I don't smoke. If I don't smoke, I don't work.' Well, do you know what they did?"

"They took the sign down," Mike said.

Corcoran looked over at him. "Did you read the book?"

"No," Mike said, and laughed. "But I'm not stupid."

"Now look," Corcoran said. "There it is. There it comes."

Mike looked closely at the test tube. There in the clear liquid floated a delicate brown ring. "Not bad," he said.

Corcoran grinned. "Nothing to it," he said. All I've got left to do now is sulfates and nickel. Listen, though, you know it's too easy when I do it myself and I know what it is I'm analyzing. How about helping me with some unknowns next week? I'll give you instructions and leave you in the lab, and when I come back you can give me five or six different things, and I'll have to find out what they are."

"Sure," Mike said. "Anything for science."

26

"You've got to learn to be more careful, though. You've got to measure from the bottom of the meniscus, like I showed you, and if it says five cc's, you can't put in seven or three. A biologist can get away with being sloppy, but chemistry is a science of *exactitude*."

"Nuts," Mike said. "Come on, let's get over to Basecamp."

Basecamp was near the east shore of the pond, about fifty yards back among some second-growth beech trees. There wasn't much to it, but the trees were the right distance apart for slinging their war-surplus jungle hammocks, and over previous summers they had made a few improvements on the site. They had stacked up stones for a fireplace and made a crude log table, binding the lengths of wood together with square lashings. Prowling the abandoned farmhouses to the south, they had scrounged up a couple of battered wooden folding chairs, a chipped enamel washbasin, and a cavernous coffeepot.

Corcoran shrugged off his pack next to where Mike had left his own, and they made camp. They slung the jungle hammocks, which had an odd smell, as if they had been impregnated with citronella. They unrolled their sleeping bags and gathered some firewood. When they had things organized, they picked up the net, the flashlight, a couple of old pillow cases they used as collecting bags, and the gas-mask bag of Mason jars to hold insect specimens, and walked down toward the pond.

At the edge of the water lay the big log, three feet thick at the butt and thirty feet long, its smaller end stretching into the water. Mike and Corcoran sat on it, side by side. Mike reached down in the leaves under the log, came up with a packet of red and white oilcloth, and unfolded it. Inside were half a dozen three-inch lengths of grapevine, and a water-repellent match case made of two shotgun shells, a 16-gauge and a 12-gauge, the smaller reversed and slipped inside the larger.

He offered Corcoran a vine, took one himself, slipped a kitchen match from the 16-gauge shell, snapped it into flame on the brass casing. Both of them lit up and dragged cautiously on the vines. The smoke was bitter, searing the tongue. Corcoran squinted in the smoke, his eyes tearing slightly. "I think these need a little more curing, Mole," he said.

For a time they sat and smoked and looked out over the smooth water, watching the dusk come on. The spring chorus of mating amphibians was already reduced from the throbbing tempo of April and May, but with the approach of darkness a sprinkling of night sounds was beginning. The twang of green frogs, the chirring notes of the cricket frogs, the occasional peeping of a hyla, and over all, the high mating trill of a lone American toad.

The pond was Mike's outdoor laboratory, his summer home; he had studied it carefully for five years now, until he knew every square foot of the bottom by heart.

He knew the deep holes where the water came in over the tops of his boots, the location of every sunken log and root mass that might trip him in the dark. He had collected, identified, and preserved, or kept alive in aquaria, specimens of virtually every nonmicroscopic creature that lived within it—227 species of insects, crustaceans, reptiles, and amphibians. Using the *Gray's Manual* in the school library, he had keyed out 27 species of trees and shrubs growing along its borders, as well as 14 species of aquatic plants. Three years ago he had stocked it with tiny bass and bluegills, the size of quarters and as bright as pennies, all seined illegally from Sandy Creek Park, and he had watched them grow into sturdy fish, the bluegills growing so fast that this spring he found them fanning their eggs in the shallows.

Corcoran came there with him often. Mike had transmitted some of his own enthusiasm, and if his friend was essentially a laboratory man, he was curious about anything that had to do with any science and learned quickly through his ferocious reading.

Now they sat together silently and watched the first little brown bat come out and flicker silently through the dusk, and then the first fireflies. The frog chorus was increasing now—that discordant symphony of moist-skinned, bug-eyed creatures, squawking and chirping and twanging their passion. The web of sound grew thicker; Mike stood up, spun the glowing end of his grapevine out into the water where it hissed into darkness. He pulled his turned-down boot tops up to his thighs, picked up his pond net. "Let's go," he said.

"Okay, *bwana*," Corcoran replied.

Side by side they walked out alongside the log into the dark water. Corcoran carried the six-volt electric lantern and had the pillowcase collecting bags looped through his belt. Mike carried the net and his gas-mask bag of bottles.

"What quarry, *bwana*?" Corcoran said softly.

"I got about all the amphibians this year," Mike said, "but I'll take a *Pseudacris triseriata* if I can get one. I caught a monster *Dytiscus* larva yesterday, the biggest one I've ever seen, and I need some tadpoles to feed him. What I'm really looking for is a big *Lethocerus*."

"The giant water bug," Corcoran said quickly.

"Hey," Mike said. "You're learning fast."

Corcoran laughed. "It's a simple science. You ought to try chemistry some time."

"How about turning on the flashlight," Mike said. "It gets deep just here."

Corcoran switched on the lantern. The powerful beam penetrated the water, revealing the world beneath the surface. The cone of light was filled with a scurry of life. Sperm-shaped tadpoles wriggled through fronds of elodea. Voracious backswimmers sculled swiftly here and there, encased in silvery bubbles of air. Crawling water beetles crept slowly along the stems of water lilies. On a submerged branch a twig swayed slightly—a water scorpion, an insect so precisely camouflaged that only its motion made it visible. There in the water lay transparent globules filled with specks of green frogs' eggs; ropy strands of toads' eggs twisted among submerged plants.

"There are plenty of tadpoles," Corcoran said quietly.

"Woodies," Mike replied. "Too little for my tiger. We'll get some big greens later. Let's press on."

For an hour they worked the pond carefully. All around them now in the dark, mating amphibians filled the night with sound, with peeping and clanging, and the vibrato trill of the toad. Corcoran skimmed the surface with the flashlight. On a floating stick a cricket frog no bigger than a thumbnail puffed the bubble of its throat until it was larger than the frog itself and chirped and sang. Mating green frogs floated silently, legs spread, male on female. A newt swam past, its feet hanging as its oarlike tail propelled it.

Mike felt the pond smell in his nose and lungs. It was a

strong smell, but not unpleasant to him. A smell of stagnant water and elodea, of last year's rotting vegetation and the spring's new growth of willow leaves and spiky cattails, of algae and mold and frogs' eggs, old life decomposing and new life swelling—a smell of life and death all mixed up together, so that he could not tell where one left off and the other began.

Within an hour Mike collected half a dozen leopard frogs for his water snakes, capturing them with his hands while Corcoran held the light on their bulging eyes. Then they found a little cove filled with fat green-frog tadpoles, and Mike captured a dozen in the net. They moved on toward the west end of the pond. The shrilling din of the pond creatures continued in uneasy rhythm, loudened, diminished, stopped dead, slowly began again. The moon glittered on the mirror surface of the water.

Corcoran, ahead of him, stopped dead still. In the center of his flashlight beam and half a dozen feet away, a gray shape hung motionless just beneath the surface. "*Tembo, bwana,*" Corcoran whispered.

The creature in the beam, two-and-a-half inches long, was the water bug Mike was seeking. In the violent, rapacious world of the pond, where even the hunters were hunted, the big water bug and the *Dytiscus,* Mike's prize of the day before, were the kings, the lions and tigers of the underwater jungle.

"Let's get him. *Kamata.* Keep the light steady. I'll take him from the side." Slowly Mike moved down the flank of the beam, careful not to break it with his shadow. When he was in reach, he slipped the bag of his net underwater with utmost caution, thus thrust forward quickly. "Hah!" he cried.

"Got him?"

"Shine the light in. Oh, yeah!" The bug squirmed in the net bag, legs and great sucking jaws all moving at once. "What a specimen," Mike said. He grinned at Corcoran. "Good work with the light," he said. "Steadfast Toad."

Back at Basecamp they built up the fire till it lit the circle of trees around them, took off their boots, and put on tennis shoes. Then Mike squatted by the fire and examined his specimens. He transferred more water into the jar containing the water bug. He popped a couple of damselfly larvae into a vial of formalin, planning to key them out later. After a while he looked up and saw Corcoran sitting staring at the flames.

"Ready to prowl?" Mike said. When they camped out like this, they rarely went to bed much before dawn. Instead, they walked for miles through the woods and empty farm fields and along the country roads, watching for meteors, discussing matters of science, and playing pranks on the inhabitants of isolated houses.

Corcoran didn't reply for a while. Finally he said, "Oh, I don't know."

"You want to eat? I've got some Dinty Moore's."

"Not yet, I guess."

He looked morose. Maybe, Mike thought, he was let down after the excitement of the hunt. "You want to go over on Blair Road and rig a spark coil to somebody's doorknob?"

"No," Corcoran said, "I'm tired of doing that."

"You always used to like it."

Corcoran looked over at him. "Mole," he said, "let's go beavershooting."

"What?"

32

"Beavershooting," Corcoran repeated.

"You're screwy," Mike said. "You know there's only muskrats here."

Corcoran shook his head. "You really are a kid sometimes."

"What are you talking about?" Mike said, irritation in his voice.

"Beavershooting," Corcoran said. "To shoot the beaver —*i.e.*, to look at a girl's beaver, *i.e.*, her pudenda and all that. Her private parts."

"Jesus!" Mike said. "You mean like a peeping tom?"

Corcoran grinned, his face vulpine in the firelight. "Roger," he said.

"Oh, come off the camel, Dickie," Mike said in exasperation. It was a line from the end of *The Light that Failed*, when young Dick Heldar, the blind correspondent, made a last heroic gesture—and got shot through the head by a Fuzzy's bullet. He and Corcoran used it whenever one felt the other was going too far.

But Corcoran just laughed. *"Foul* Toad," he said. *"Filthy* Toad. *Obscene* Toad." He sighed, looked over at Mike. "Boy," he said, "you know, all I think about anymore is breasts. All I think about is Marilyn Bishop's Lucky Strikes, so round, so firm, so fully packed, so free and easy on the draw. I work in my lab and I look at an Erlenmeyer flask, and you know what I think about?— knockers, that's what. I think I'm becoming a knocker fiend. I even think about my stupid big sister's knockers. I just want to run barefoot through a field of boobs."

"I know what you mean," Mike said.

"Let's go, then."

"Go where?"

"Let's go down by your place, by Karmans'. Angeline ought to be going to bed about now, and there's a lot of trees you can climb around there."

"Angeline?" Mike said.

"Well, she doesn't have half as much as Marilyn, but she's the only girl who lives close, and she sure is pointy."

"Angeline?" Mike said.

"Pointy like ice-cream cones," Corcoran said, jumping to his feet. He clasped his hands to his chest and staggered forward. "I fall upon the ice-cream cones of life, I bleed," he yelled, and pitched forward on his face. Then he rolled over. "Aieeeee!" he yowled.

"Oh, for crying out loud," Mike said.

"Watch that branch," Corcoran said from above him. "It doesn't feel solid."

"*Acer rubrum,*" Mike said to Corcoran's feet. "Red maple—kind of brittle."

"Let go of my leg."

"Your cuff is caught on a branch, clumsy Toad. O.K., you're loose now."

Corcoran moved a little higher in the tree, Mike following him limb by limb.

"You sure this is her room, here in the back?"

"I don't know. It used to be, when we were little. We played there when we were kids."

"The light's on, but nobody's in there. Wait a minute— it must be her room, there's about a dozen pictures of Elizabeth Taylor on the wall."

"How about moving your foot so I can get up there."

"These branches are getting kind of small."

"*I'm* the one who knew what room it was."

34

"Okay, but be careful. Don't stand on this one I'm standing on."

Mike squeezed himself upward. Corcoran said, "Do you think they're real?"

"The branches?"

"Her knockers, cretinous Mole. Maybe she wears falsies."

"Look, how about moving your feet? I can't get up to see over the windowsill."

"Oh," Corcoran said. "Oh, boy."

"What is it?"

"She's there. She just came in." Looking up, Mike saw a shadow cross the window above the level of the sill.

"She's wearing a bathrobe, though," Corcoran said.

"Look, how about moving your big feet?"

"Holy cow! She's taking it off, Mole. Holy *cow*."

"What is it?"

"Ohhhhh," Corcoran moaned. "There they are!"

"I can't *see*," Mike whispered fiercely. *"I can't get past your damn feet."*

"Ahhhhh," Corcoran gasped. Then he said quickly, "No, Mike, wait a minute—boy, this branch won't hold both . . ."

The branch split with a sharp crack. Mike jerked downward, crashing into the other branches a few feet below. He fetched up on his back, cradled in the vee formed by two big branches. Straight above his head, Corcoran's feet kicked in midair as he dangled from a handhold. Corcoran locked his legs around the tree trunk, peered down like a lemur. The bedroom light switched off.

"Shit," Corcoran said. "What did you do that for?"

"Shush," Mike whispered. Below him he heard the

screen door of the house swing upon its long spring. Afraid to move, he swiveled his eyes around in his head and saw the squat, anthropoid shape of Mr. Karman move out onto the back steps and into the moonlight. He was wearing only his pants and an undershirt. Mike glanced up quickly —Corcoran was frozen absolutely still, his eyes goggling, pasted to the treetrunk like a gecko on a wall. Mike swiveled his eyes down again. Karman came down the steps, stood at the foot of them, and peered up into the tree. After a moment he bent down, fumbled around in his wife's flower bed, stood erect again. A moment later a clod of earth whistled through the leaves a foot from Mike's head.

"You!" Karman said loudly.

Mike stopped breathing. His body felt immobile as a slab of concrete. Above him, Corcoran's eyes got even wider, and his mouth had gone all funny.

"You!" Karman said from below. Another clod of earth shot through the leaves and atomized against the tree trunk, spraying Mike's face with dirt.

"You—racoon! Stay out the tomatoes!"

Afterward, they walked. They crossed the forest by moonlight, with Mike, a little more certain in the woods, leading the way beneath the overarching beeches and maples. They crossed the farm fields to the south, making a glistening trail through the dew-wet grass, past the abandoned farmhouses and dilapidated barns. They walked for miles along the country roads, slipping silently into the roadside brush when a rare, lone car passed by. Normally they chattered to each other on these nocturnal rambles, Corcoran expounding on his latest theories of perpetual motion and extrasensory perception, Mike talking about the taxonomy of accipitrine hawks and the adventures of Theodore Roosevelt and his son Kermit. But tonight they talked little, Mike sensing that Corcoran felt subdued and feeling subdued himself.

Once, cutting along a fence line, they surprised a baby skunk, its mother nowhere in sight. It stamped its feet, raised its tail harmlessly, too young a kitten to be armed with scent. Standing its ground as it did, it would have been easy enough to capture, but neither Mike nor Corcoran moved to do so. They simply stood and watched until the little creature lowered its tail and waddled into the cover along the fence.

When their legs began to feel weary and the late night dampness began to chill them through their clothes, they turned back toward camp, trudging silently under the wheeling moon. When they were almost due south of the pond, they cut cattycorner across an abandoned field. Mike realized after a moment that he was walking not through tall grass but on slick, bare earth. "What's this?" he said. Corcoran stopped beside him. Ahead of them the naked earth, glinting softly in the moonlight, ran back a hundred yards toward the trees. "Maybe somebody's farming here again," Mike said. He didn't like that idea much. The old field had been one of his favorite collecting spots, a place where he could always kick up a garter snake and, with luck, a blue racer. For the past two years he had seeded the field with old pieces of roofing and tar paper from the collapsing barn; the cover they provided attracted snakes like flies to sugar, and by patrolling the fields, turning over one piece after another, he could usually come up with a good mixed bag—he even hoped he might get a copperhead there someday.

Now Mike looked across the field toward the old farmhouse to see if it showed any new signs of occupancy. "That's funny," he said.

"What's funny?"

"I don't see the farmhouse. With the moon this bright we ought to be able to see it against the trees. Let's go on over there."

They walked for a hundred yards in the direction of the farmhouse and found it, finally, but it was not a house anymore, just a great stack of boards and joists and shingles heaped up next to the gaping hole that had once been the cellar.

"I wonder what happened?" Mike said.

"What's that over there?"

"Where?"

"By the trees—that lightish patch. Something's over there."

"Let's take a look."

"Wow!" Corcoran said softly a few minutes later. "Wow!"

They stood staring up at a great yellow machine. It was the biggest bulldozer Mike had ever seen, square and massive as an iron mastodon. At the front end of the thing a gleaming blade stretched up far higher than Mike could reach. Along the top of the hood someone had painted, crudely and in large letters, the word PUSSYCAT.

"What do you suppose it's doing here?" Mike said.

Corcoran shrugged. "Maybe they're going to build some new houses."

"It sure messed up a good snake field," Mike said.

Corcoran walked around the side of the beast. After a moment he stepped forward and began to climb it, like a man scaling a cliff. Eventually he reached the summit, slid onto the seat, peered down at Mike.

"Come on up," he said.

Mike scrambled up over the earth-clotted tracks, ascended the body, finally reached the seat and slid onto it next to Corcoran. The bulldozer was different from any machine he had ever seen before. There was no wheel in front of him, just a bewildering assemblage of levers and pedals. Looking down, Mike felt as if he were a captain on the bridge of a ship.

Corcoran reached forward and put his hands on a couple of the levers. Mike expected him to try to find out how to start the machine—he couldn't stand not knowing how something worked—but a moment later he released the levers and slumped back on the broad seat.

"You bring any grapevines, Mike?" he asked.

"Yeah," Mike said. He got them out and the shotgun shell of matches. They lit up and sat there in the moonlight, smoking the bitter vine, not talking.

After a long time Mike said, "John."

"Yes?"

"What did she look like?"

Corcoran didn't answer right away. He let out a little sigh. Then he said, "They were beautiful, Mike."

"You would probably be surprised," Mike read in Lord Baden-Powell's scout manual, "if you knew how many boys have written to me thanking me for what I have written on this subject, so I expect there are more who will be glad of a word of advice against the secret vice which gets hold of so many fellows. Smoking and drinking and gambling are men's vices and therefore attract some boys, but this secret vice is not a man's vice—men have nothing but contempt for a fellow who gives way to it."

"Oh, boy," said Mike. He read on: ". . . the reading of trashy books or looking at lewd pictures are very apt to lead a thoughtless boy into the temptation of self-abuse.

This is a most dangerous thing for him, for, should it become a habit, it tends to lower both health and spirits."

Mike sighed, looked up from the book and out the window and up the hill toward Karman's house. Angeline was nowhere in sight. He sighed again.

"Sometimes," he read on, "the desire is brought on by indigestion, or from eating too rich food, or from constipation, or from sleeping in too warm a bed with too many blankets."

"Constipation?" Mike said aloud. "Indigestion?"

"If you still have trouble about it," he read, "do not make a secret of it, but go to your father, or your Scoutmaster, and talk it over with him, and all will come right."

He closed the book. "Oh, for crying out loud," he said. Did Kermit Roosevelt have the secret vice, he wondered? Did Kermit talk it over with *his* father?

Restless, he got up and started to move around the room, assembling his collecting gear: the insect net; his killing jar, in the bottom a piece of cotton doused with Carbona cleaning fluid; a nosedrop bottle filled with Carbona (to pacify stinging insects before removing them from the net); a Boy Scout knife with lots of blades; two pairs of hemostats for picking things up; Lutz's *Field Guide to the Insects*; four small vials of formalin for pickling things; two oxygen tabs; a pocket magnifier; a pair of tweezers; a Prince Albert tobacco can full of cotton in case he found a nest. As he began stuffing these odds and ends into the gas-mask bag, Andy entered the room, stood there sniffing. "Something dead in here?" he said. He walked over to the workbench, picked up a cast-off snakeskin, sniffed at it, picked up a pair of scissors, sniffed them.

41

"How about laying off smelling everything," Mike said. "And you've got your shirt buttoned up wrong."

Andy put down the scissors, started to unbutton his shirt. "Where are you going, up to your pond?" Mike nodded. "How about taking your little brother along? There's nothing to do around this place."

"I've got some serious collecting to do, and you always get bored up there and want to come home."

"So, I don't need you to come home."

"Come on," Mike said, "you always get scared when you're in the woods by yourself."

"I do not."

"You're doing it wrong again. Get the top button in the top buttonhole."

Andy rebuttoned his shirt again, picked up the shell of a cicada larva, smelled it. "Big brothers are supposed to take their little brothers places. You know the Indians are playing today, we could go downtown to the ball game."

"I've got too much to do," Mike said. "Besides, I haven't got any money."

"You got some paper-route money. I can get some money off Dad; it was payday yesterday."

"Look, I'm busy," Mike said. "I'm just about out of food for my collection."

He leaned over and peered into the battery jar where the big water tiger hung immobile.

"Hannibal hasn't had a tadpole in two days. And the old Nilghai needs some sowbugs."

"Oh, all you care about is your smelly old bugs and worms." Andy turned and walked out, stamping his feet down the hall.

Mike looked at himself in the mirror, turned the collar of his shirt up in back on the chance that Angeline might see him as he walked up the hill, picked up his gear, and left the house. A few minutes later, passing the barn, he saw a pair of legs sticking out from under the Fordson. Next to the Cadillac, the Fordson was his father's greatest love. During the war years when people were raising victory gardens, his father had bought the ancient tractor for fifteen dollars and had spent all of his weekends for two months getting the thing to run. Then he scrounged up a rusty harrow and plow and, with his natural instinct for overdoing things, plowed the entire east field and planted it with tomatoes. He hadn't the foggiest notion how many tomatoes so many plants would produce— he probably visualized a crop of a few pecks. As it turned out, the entire family spent its summer evenings vainly trying to keep up with the harvesting. They ate tomatoes till they grew sick of them; his father took bushel baskets of them to work to give away, his mother spent all day canning them, Mike sold them up and down 196th Street for twenty cents a peck, the raccoons came down out of the woods and ate them off the vines, and one evening in late August his father, sweaty from the field, came into the kitchen, opened a bottle of beer, and said: "Martha, I get the feeling that there is this big mountain of tomatoes out there in the field that's just going to go up like a volcano one of these days and bury us all under tomatoes." By the end of the summer, none of them ever wanted to see another tomato. After that his father's attempts at victory gardening were less ambitious. By then he realized that he really hated farming, but he still loved to drive the tractor, and on Saturdays and Sundays he would sometimes hire himself and the Fordson out to anyone who had a patch of ground he wanted plowed.

As Mike passed, his father slid out from under the tractor, wiped grease from his hands. "Hi," he said.

"Fixing the tractor?"

"I think I have to replace a bearing."

Mike nodded, somewhat uncertain what a bearing was. "You going off collecting?"

"Yes, to the pond."

The man looked at him for a moment.

"Well," he said, "I'm tired of lying under this infernal machine. We haven't spent much time together lately. Maybe I'll go along with you. If you don't mind."

"Sure," Mike said. "I mean, sure, I don't mind."

Side by side they walked up through the field. There was a rustle behind them. Bozo, the family's fumble-footed springer spaniel, came bouncing up, ears flapping, his big feet going in four different directions.

"Oh, Okay, come along, Wolf," Mike said, "but for crying out loud, keep out of the pond."

The dog settled in at his father's heels. "How come you call him Wolf?" his father asked.

"How can you call a dog Bozo?" Mike said. "What sort of name is that?"

"Well, seems to me it suits him, son. He hasn't eaten anybody lately."

"Wolves *don't* eat people," Mike said. "There has never been a substantiated case of a wolf eating a human being."

His father laughed. "There has never been a substantiated case of a slobber-tongued dog like that being called Wolf, either. If that dog is a wolf, I'm a—I'm a *Tyrannosaurus rex.*"

44

Mike looked up at his father. "Where'd you learn about them?"

"Even old folks know some things," the man said.

When they reached the pond, they sat down on the log while Mike organized his gear. "Listen," the man said. "I want to ask you something." Mike waited. "Mike, have you been smoking grapevines?"

"Who told you that?"

"Never mind about that. Have you?"

"Andy told you. It must have been Andy."

His father started to say something, closed his mouth, looked at him sternly.

"Well, just once in a while," Mike said. "Not so often."

"How do you do it?"

"You just cut them off and dry them and smoke them."

"I'd like to try it," the man said.

"You want to smoke a *grapevine*?"

"Son, if you're going to smoke grapevines, I want to know what it's like."

"Keeripes," Mike said. "Okay, if you want to." He dug down under the log, got the oil cloth packet. "I keep a few here," he said. He gave one of the vine lengths to the man.

"How do I do it?"

"You just light it and smoke it like a cigarette." Mike opened the shotgun shells, flicked a match against the brass of the shell, puffed his own vine into flame, blew out a mouthful of acrid smoke, held the match out to his father. The man took three or four puffs, then, when the end began to glow, he took a long, thoughtful drag—and burst into a paroxysm of coughing. His face grew red, tears streamed down his cheeks.

45

"You can't *inhale* it," Mike said. "I forgot to tell you . . ." His voice trailed off.

The man wheezed. He breathed cautiously a few times, tears still running from his eyes. "Jesus H. Christ," he gasped. When he got his breathing under control, he shook his head. "When I was a kid, everyone smoked corn silk. I'll tell you, it's a lot easier to take than this. But as long as you don't inhale it, I guess it can't do you too much harm."

For a while the two sat on the log in silence. Then his father said, "Well, I think I've got my design for the Draft-eez perfected. And I've got my patent application in."

"That's swell, Dad."

The man grinned at him. "We might not get porter-house steak three times a day and move to Shaker Heights like your mother says, but I just don't see how this one is going to miss. This time I'm going to be smart. The last two designs I did, I needed the money and I sold my rights for a few hundred bucks, but I'm not going to get shy-stered like that this time. I'm going to get some investors, some backers, and set up a little company and manufac-ture them and sell them myself. So if anybody is going to make money, it will be me."

"It would be bully to be rich," Mike said.

"It sure would." His father grinned.

They sat silently again, looking out over the pond. Then the man began hesitantly, "Well, you're getting pretty grown-up now, Mike."

"I guess so," Mike said.

"I suppose you're starting to get interested in girls."

"Well, they're all right."

"That little Angeline Karman up the hill, she's cute as

a bug's ear. She looks sort of like that little girl from *National Velvet*—that Elizabeth Taylor."

"I guess she's O.K." Mike felt himself flushing.

"I thought maybe we ought to have a little talk," the man said. "I mean, you're probably going to start going out on dates pretty soon, and I thought maybe there were, ah, some things we ought to talk about."

Mike felt his ears burning. Was his father going to ask him about the secret vice? Did he *know*?

"Hey, look out there," Mike said abruptly.

"What?"

"There, just out from the end of the pond. Two painted turtles, *Chrysemys picta*."

"Oh, yes, one is on top of the other one. Riding piggyback."

"They're copulating," Mike said.

"They're copulating?" his father said. "Oh, I see, you mean—yes, I see." He stood up for a better view. The turtles disappeared in a swirl of brown water.

"Oh, nuts," Mike said. "You scared them."

"I'm sorry," the man said. "I didn't mean"—he laughed—"I didn't mean to interrupt them. But—how do they do it actually? Ah, copulate?"

Mike sighed. "Well, the female just lies there and the male sits on her back, and he kind of wraps his tail around hers and puts his penis into her cloaca."

"I see," the man said.

"The reptiles have intercourse," Mike said. "Lizards can do it. Snakes can do it. Turtles can do it. But the amphibia can't do it. With frogs and toads the female just lays her eggs, and the male puts his sperm on top of them."

47

"I'll be damned," his father said, and laughed. "I'm glad I'm not a frog. I'd rather be a turtle."

Mike giggled. "You mean you want to try it with a turtle?"

"I guess not," the man said. "Not with a snapping turtle anyway." The two of them laughed together then; and afterward the man said, "Well, I was going to tell you something, but never mind. It isn't always easy to tell you things, Mike. Why don't you go ahead and do your collecting. I'll just sit here and watch." He grinned. "Maybe I'll smoke a few grapevines."

For the next half hour Mike worked his way through the pond, while his father sat sunning on the log like an old terrapin and the dog splashed clumsily in the shallows. It was pleasantly warm wading in the pond. Frogs twanged softly from time to time. Once Mike heard a high-pitched, mechanical stutter coming from the woods south of the pond, and he paused and listened, puzzled. After a moment the sound settled to a distant rumble, and he realized that it must be the bulldozer he had seen.

He returned to his collecting, and when he had a jar full of tadpoles, a week's food for Hannibal, he rejoined his father on the log. "Sounds like a D-model back there," Mr. Harrington said.

"A big bulldozer has been working the last couple of weeks over near the county road," Mike said. "It messed up a pretty good snake field."

"Let's go take a look," the man said.

They walked over through the woods, the dog flopping behind, Mike feeling oddly companionable. "You see those over there?" He pointed to the three thick-boled oaks. "They are Moses Cleaveland trees. They're over 150

48

years old. I measured them and sent in the information to the Sesquicentennial Commission, and they sent me little brass plaques to put on them."

"Really?" his father said. "I didn't know there were any trees that old around here. I'd like to see them."

They walked over to the trees, and his father leaned down to look at the plaque on the first one. "Isn't that something?" he said. "You ought to feel proud of that."

"I had to measure them," Mike said. "And calculate how tall they are."

"How did you do that?" the man asked. "The height?"

"It's easy," Mike said. "You pound a stick in the ground. You measure the stick, then you measure its shadow. Then you pace off the shadow of the tree. The ratio between the shadow of the stick and the shadow of the tree is the same as the ratio between the height of the stick and the height of the tree."

His father grinned. "Yes, that's right, that's just how you could do it. I never thought about it, but that would be a very good way of solving that problem. That's pretty good. And I thought math was one thing you didn't like."

"Corcoran helped me," Mike admitted. "He's really good at it."

"But you understand the principle now," his father said. "You know, that's like the kind of thing I do at work every day. The problems I have to work on are harder than that one, but it's the same kind of thing."

They walked on toward the sound of the bulldozer, Mike flushing a little from the praise. After a bit they came out of the woods, and there was the machine, a hundred yards closer to the trees than it had been a week ago,

49

lurching against a mound of earth and dead brush it had piled up, clanking back, lurching forward again.

"Look at that," the man said as they walked closer. "It *is* a D-Model, the new one we just brought out. She's got a Hercules DRXB, McCord tube and fin radiator, double-plate clutch, force-feed lubrication. She'll move a house."

They stood watching. Mike had to admit that the machine was stirring; there was a kind of excitement in its mass, its raw power. Blade lowered, it rammed forward again, this time shoving the pile of earth and uprooted trees ten feet ahead. When the machine backed off, the operator looked down, noticed them, nodded, then tilted his hat back on his head, killed the roaring engine. The silence was a blow on the ears.

"How you doing?" his father said.

The man grinned. "Hot work." He took his straw hat off, dragged his sleeve across his face. He was a heavyset man, and his moon face was lit up by his thinning hair, red below from the sun.

"Got an Atlas D there, huh?" Mike's father asked.

"Yeah," the man said. He reached behind him in the cab, came up with a bottle of water, took a swig. "Sweet machine," he said.

"I work on them," Mr. Harrington said. "Not on the dozers themselves. I work on the conveyors for the line at the plant."

"You did a good job on this one," the man said. "I've skinned Cletracks, Caterpillars, and Euclids, but this is the best machine I've skinned yet."

"How's that radiator—she overheat on you at all?"

"She'll purr in a hundred degrees." He waved his hand

toward the crude lettering on the hood. "That's why I named her Pussycat, 'cause she purrs all the time. She'll go when I'd rather not. I hope it cools off tomorrow."

"You've got about three more days of hot weather coming," Mike informed the man. "You see that high cirrus up there?" He pointed to the lacy clouds above. "That's generally a sign of a warm front coming. It'll rain in a couple of days, though."

The man stared down at him. His father said, "This is my son, Mike. He's quite an expert on weather and things like that."

The man smiled. "Glad to meet you," he said.

"What are you building here?" Mike asked.

"There's a new housing development going in here," the man said. "I'm clearing the land. Gonna put in a bunch of new houses."

"That'll make a mess of my pond," Mike said. "A lot of people messing around. That's all I need. I have this pond," he explained. "It's kind of my laboratory."

"Well, I don't know," the man said. "I'm only clearing north to the crest of the hill."

That took a moment to sink in. Mike couldn't register it for a moment. His father and the man were talking on, their mouths moving, the sun high in the sky, the dozer operator mopping his brow.

"The crest of the hill?" Mike yelled. "My pond is back there! What about my pond?"

"Yeah, they told me there was some kind of swamp back there," the man said. "I haven't seen it yet. I guess I'll have to cut a channel so she drains, then fill it in."

"Fill it in?"

"With this baby, it's not hard to do," the man said. "I

hear there's some big trees back there too, but you can't show me a stump I can't pull."

"The trees? Those are my Moses Cleaveland trees! They are registered with the Sesquicentennial Commission."

The man stared at him. "I don't care who they're registered with, son, my orders are to clear 'em out. We got a big project going in here. The boss plans on a couple of hundred homes eventually—of course, we can't do all that at once." He pointed out toward the east. "See, we're going that way as far as Elm Lane." He swiveled on his seat and pointed back toward the west. "And out that way along the county road. And let me tell you, as soon as lumber prices get down a little more, we're gonna start throwing those houses up. Hasn't been a new house around here for five years, and, boy, are they gonna sell."

"But that's the whole woods," Mike said. He could hardly hear his voice. "That's the whole thing."

"You bet your britches," the man said.

For the next few days Mike spent a great deal of time in the woods, but he felt aimless, drifting. He didn't collect much of anything. His senses were so dulled by his preoccupation that one evening he almost stepped on a possum before he saw it—Kermit would hardly have approved. He went to see Toad, who was sympathetic but so excited by a scheme for a new perpetual-motion machine that he was of no help. A couple of times he lurked behind a screen of brush and watched the bulldozer working, steadily enlarging its clearing, chomping at the leafy borders of the field like a hungry elephant.

Finally, Mr. Karman lost another chicken and brought

home an old 12-gauge shotgun he'd bought secondhand, and that, at least, gave Mike a problem he could try to do something about. He was determined to talk the man out of shooting the red-tailed hawks. They had been around for three or four years, and each summer he had watched them cutting their long, gentle circles way up over the fields and woods, tilting over on their wide wings so the sun glinted on the rusty fans of their tails. They were beautiful birds, thick plumaged, graceful as sloops, with strong hooked beaks and dark eyes, and sometimes they would rise on afternoon thermals until they were almost invisible, then come gliding and slipping down again, their screams so high-pitched and fierce that they made you shiver. Earlier in the year Mike had searched for their nest, hoping he could get a young one to train as a hunting hawk, but he had had no success and realized that he was probably too late now, for the young would be almost fully fledged.

Redtails were rodent-eaters mostly, and Mike felt quite certain that they weren't taking Karman's chickens —probably a fox, or maybe a little Cooper's hawk was guilty of that—but he couldn't break through Karman's encrustation of ignorance, which held that since he'd always heard hawks called chicken hawks, they must eat chickens.

So in the warmth of one afternoon, Mike lay back of an osage hedge in the woods up behind Karman's house, passing the time by reading from John Bichard May's *The Hawks of North America*. Karman had avoided him for a couple of days, and Mike had decided that if he wanted to do any further lobbying he would have to resort to ambush.

It was an hour before he heard something moving and looked up to see Karman swinging down the path through the woods, carrying a peck basket in each hand. Mike popped up and stepped through the screen of osage into the path. "Ai!" the man yelped, startled, and gave a little skip and jump, then stood there in the middle of the path, glaring. "What you do?" he said.

"I was just waiting for you," Mike said.

The man eyed him warily, noting the volume under his arm. "Don't read no more the book," he said, and swung past Mike and on down the path. Mike caught up, walked along beside. "What did you get?" he asked, looking down at the baskets in Karman's hands. Whatever they contained was covered with pieces of cloth.

"Moshroom," Karman said.

"I found out how you tell," Mike said. When the man just kept walking, Mike said, "You make sure they haven't got a volva, or else any floccose patches.

"That's little bits of stuff," he added a moment later. "Floccose is."

"How you find out that?" Karman said.

"In the library, in a book on fungi. On mushrooms."

Karman said nothing, and Mike asked, "That's how you tell, isn't it?"

"You tell the book way," Karman said. "I tell my way. You eat the book moshroom, I eat my moshroom."

As they reached the garden behind Karman's house, Mike took *The Hawks of North America* from under his arm and opened it to a place he'd marked. "I just found something new here."

"Don't read no more the book."

"I just thought you might want to know," Mike said,

55

"that in a stomach contents' analysis by W. L. McAtee of 750 redtail stomachs, mammal remains were found in 650, among which were 385 mice. Only 86 showed poultry-game bird remains. Thus, mammals comprised 86 percent of the food and birds 12 percent."

"Let alone with the book," said Karman, and began walking faster.

Mike stretched out his stride to keep up. "Chickens," he read aloud, "always easy prey and taken largely by immature hawks, plus quail, grouse, and ducks, are taken *occasionally*. It is well to remember, in this connection, that cripples and even dead birds are eaten now and then, so that it is not correct to assume that such remains found in the stomachs necessarily mean that the hawk in question took healthy or living birds."

"You walking in my cucumber," said Karman.

Mike stopped, looked down, disentangled his feet from the cucumber plant, hurried to catch up again. "I'll bet it's a fox," he said.

Karman stopped dead and turned toward him, his arms drooping like a chimp's. "Look," he said. "Look, smart kid. I see no fox here for two, three year. I see no hole in fence. Instead," and he raised one arm, still holding the basket of mushrooms, straight over his head and pointed his index finger at the sky, "I see that one. So don't tell me." He dropped his arm, turned on his heel, and marched off toward the house, leaving Mike standing there amid the cucumbers with *The Hawks of North America* open in his hand.

Karman shot the first of the redtails two days later, early in the afternoon. Mike was in the woodshed, cleaning his cages, when he heard the deep thump of the shotgun. By the time he got outside he saw the man walking across his fields with the gun over his shoulder, pulling the hawk behind him by one wing, the other dragging among the broccoli. The other redtail circled above, screaming wildly, high enough to be out of range.

By the time Mike reached the chicken coop, the hawk had been nailed, wings outstretched, to the weathered gray boards. The soft white underwings stretched almost five feet across the old boards, and the body hung limp from them, the rusty tail fanned out, and a drop of blood started from the hooked beak. Karman stood a few feet back on the bare earth of the chicken yard, holding a hammer and regarding the hawk. The leghorns were clumped in a far corner, milling nervously.

Mike walked over to the hawk, touched the soft feathers of its breast. After a moment he said, "That was really a stupid thing to do."

Karman stood there with the hammer in his hand, looking uncomfortable. "I have to get other one too," he said.

"Sure," Mike said.

"Sorry, but I can't afford lose more chicken."

"Sure," Mike said.

Karman put his own hand on the bird's breast. Against the creamy feathers his fingers were dark and knotty, with dirt rammed under the battered fingernails.

"Pretty, huh?" he said. "I never shoot hawk before." He turned then and picked up his shotgun and walked away across the field, the gun looking heavy in his hand.

Mike squatted down in the dust by the chicken house, and for a while he looked up at the hawk draped on the wall in front of him. Once he heard the bird's mate screaming and turned his head to see it circling high above the field to the west. It was safe now, disturbed and staying high, but in a day or two it would be hunting the fields again, and sooner or later it would come within range of Karman's shotgun.

It was the following day before he found the fox tracks, or what he thought were fox tracks, indistinct impressions in soft earth only twenty yards behind the chicken house. Kneeling on the ground, he searched for the sign of the arched bar on the heel pad that foxes possess, but dogs do not, and thought he saw its faint outline. That night he said he was going camping with Corcoran again, and not long after dark he sat down under a tree in a position that gave him a good view of the chicken house, wrapped his sleeping bag around his shoulders, and waited.

The darkness, in the hours before the moon rising, was so heavy that the only stimuli were sounds. Cicadas made their thick churr; he heard the trill of a screech owl once, and the high, mysterious buzzing of the nighthawks as they patrolled the dark sky, and from way up in the woods, the faint sound of the hylas peeping. At Karman's house across the fields he saw the downstairs lights go out. But the light in Angeline's bedroom stayed on for a while, and he could hear the sounds of polka music drifting through the open window. The light went off eventually. He pulled the sleeping bag closer around his shoulders and settled his back against the tree and stared into the darkness until colored lights the shape of paramecia spun and pirouetted inside his skull.

He stood looking across the tundra. It rolled like the sea toward the horizon where the Brooks Range stood

58

jagged and white against sky; the land was open, limitless, yellowish brown except for the patches of snowdrifts and the darker slashes of dwarf willow and birch. Far off, almost at the limit of his own sharp vision, the faint dark specks of the caribou herd moved almost imperceptibly against the landscape. The great wolf stirred beside him, its muzzle lifted to the wind.

"Easy, big fellow," he said, and looked down into the yellow, Asian eyes that shone with loyalty and affection. "Easy," he said again. "There'll be time."

On his left wrist the white gyrfalcon shifted its yellow talons, turned its head to look at him, the question in its great eyes. He caressed the falcon's snowy breast with his fingers, feeling through the feathers the fast, fierce beating of the heart. He chuckled. "Easy, my loves, my brave hunters," he said. "Tonight we must rest. Tomorrow we will kill."

Later, in the rude cabin, he sat before the fire, carefully oiling the rifle, the .450 magnum. The wolf lay beside him, its muzzle resting on the toe of his boot. On its perch in the corner, the gyr slept quietly, its head drawn beneath its wing. A knock came on the door. When he opened it, she was standing there in the moonlight, her white bobby socks gleaming softly. "Come in," he said graciously. "You must pardon this humble dwelling, but there are only the three of us, my wolf, my gyr, and myself, and I am afraid we live rather crudely, for we so rarely have visitors. You are, in fact, the first human being we have seen in three years. Perhaps you would like a cup of tea?"

She entered hesitantly. Her eyes, wide with apprehension, were fixed upon the wolf, who stood erect and alert now. "Don't be afraid," he reassured her. "Wolf would never harm you. At a single command from me he would, of course, attack a lion, but you need not fear him, for he knows that you are my friend."

Later, after he had fixed her a supper of caribou and the breast of a willow ptarmigan the gyr had killed that morning, she sat at his feet on the polar bear rug in front of the warm fire, while he told her more of his adventures.

"But where did you come from?" she said.

"Some years back," he explained, "we crossed the Bering Sea on the ice from Siberia. We had one touchy moment with a polar bear, Thalarctos, but Wolf attacked him fearlessly and held him at bay until I could get a good shot with the magnum. That's his fur you're sitting on."

"It's beautiful," she said. "But I don't see a bullet hole."

He shrugged. "I got him through the eye," he said. "I hate to deface a good hide."

"But will you always live like this?" she asked. "Here, so far from civilization."

He looked slowly around the room, at his rifle, his snowshoes, his rude possessions. "Yes," he said softly. "Here, alone, with my hunters, I shall never—return to the world."

"You know I cannot stay," she said. Her eyes were bright with tears. "There's a dance at school next week."

"I know," he said.

She lifted her soft, delicate hand and placed it on his strong brown one. The fire pickled russet highlights in her dark hair. "I'll never forget you," she said.

Mike opened his eyes. A half moon had risen, illuminating the fields with a light that seemed almost phosphorescent. It had grown colder, and he shivered, pulled the sleeping bag closer around his shoulders. He looked up at the open sky beyond the branches above him. It was about two, he judged, from the position of Sagittarius. "You had better stay awake now," he told himself. "You'll miss him if you keep daydreaming."

It was about an hour later that the fox appeared. There was nothing there, then suddenly something was, a dark shape moving against the fence a dozen yards from him. Mike gasped, clamped his lips together. *He's climbing it*, he said inside his head. *He's climbing the fence!* And indeed, the fox was climbing the vertical chicken-wire fence, placing his paws through the holes in the wire, as surely as a man would climb a ladder. It's got to be a cat, he thought, a fox couldn't do that. But he could see the animal clearly enough in the moonlight, and the heavy brush was plain. It was a fox, all right.

Then, quickly, it was over the top, across the moonlit yard, and lost in the shadows of the building itself. He expected a wild uproar, a chicken volcano, but there was just a momentary clucking and a squawk from inside the building, and then silence. A few moments later the fox materialized from the shadows again, dragging something white. The fox moved quickly down to the other end of the building, where Karman had left a stack of old boards and joists, the jettison of some partitions he'd rebuilt. The fox scrambled among the lumber, and in a moment he had reached the building's low roof and was trotting back along it. When he reached the end near Mike, he hesitated for a moment, then leapt lightly from the roof to the ground, not letting go of his prey. Then he went trotting up the hill behind the chicken house, and in a moment disappeared into the brush.

"Oh, boy," Mike said softly but aloud. "That old man is *never* going to believe this."

At first light he started trying to track the fox. He would have to find the den, he thought, and see if he could retrieve some chicken remains, for without something in the way of evidence, Karman would think the story a lie. He began on the hill behind the chicken house while Karman's cocks were yawping at the dawn, and although he found one or two white feathers where they had stuck on a blackberry bush, the ground was covered with brush and a mulch of last year's fallen leaves, and the light animal left no trail that he could discern. By the time the sun was up, he realized that he had no hope whatsoever of tracking the animal to its den. His only chance, a remote one, was in quartering the woods thoroughly, checking out anything that looked like a possible den site for signs of digging or chicken feathers, and hoping that sooner or later, if the fox was not traveling too great a distance, he would stumble on the den.

On the first day he thrashed about in the woods till noon, checking around the roots of larger trees, pushing his way into blackberry brambles at the edge of clearings, snaking through a grove of young, thorny honey locusts. By noon he was red-eyed, sleepy, bleeding from half a dozen scratches, and hungry. He had seen three rabbits, two red squirrels, found some possum tracks in a marshy place, but no sign of a fox. He went home for lunch, turned aside his mother's questions, and afterwards went back up the hill with the springer spaniel, which he secured by a leash just in case, in hunting fervor, the dog took off down the trail at a pace faster than Mike could follow.

"There he is, Wolf," Mike said, drawing the dog's attention to the bramble on which the feathers had caught. "He went right by here. Get a good smell of him. Let's go, big fellow."

The dog stared at him dolefully. "Come on, Wolf," he said, and snapped the leash.

The spaniel yawned. "Oh, come on," Mike said. He grabbed the dog by the neck, forced his nose down to the ground by the bush. The spaniel's nostrils quivered; his nose began to vacuum around among the leaves. "Attaboy," Mike said, and gave the dog a slap on the rump. Feet flailing, the dog took off, downhill. "Wait!" Mike yelled, but the big springer didn't wait, he charged ahead, Mike dragging behind, until he fetched up against the wire of the chicken house. On the other side of the wire one of the white leghorn roosters erected its comb and went into an aggression display. The dog barked furiously at it, then, obviously pleased with himself, looked up at Mike and wagged his tail.

"Nuts," Mike said.

On the second day he searched again, getting down on his hands and knees to peer into hollow logs, poking about rock outcroppings along the ravines. At about three in the afternoon, he worked the borders of the abandoned farm where he and Corcoran had found the bulldozer. From the edge of the woods he could see that the area of bare earth was larger now, and after a moment he saw the bulldozer itself, far across the fields, sitting still and quiet and gleaming yellow. Methodically, he began to walk along the woodline, and suddenly the fox was there in front of him, not more than thirty feet away. It was standing in some low grass, side on to him, a big dog of an animal, magnificently furred with a reddish coat shading to black over its shoulders and a full, white-tipped brush. For a moment it stared straight at him from its intelligent eyes, and looking into them Mike felt almost as if he could see the wheels turning inside the animal's brain. After a moment the fox turned and trotted away, moving with a precision that was almost dainty, not hurried in the least, but with the leisurely arrogance of a terminal predator.

"Aren't you a beauty," Mike gasped.

And the fox was gone. Just like that.

He must, Mike reasoned, be close to the den. The fox wouldn't likely be far afield in the full glare of the afternoon. He started to search, looking first at likely cover, but he found nothing. After an hour he returned to the spot where he had seen the fox and started a spiral search, trying to keep each whorl not more than ten yards from the preceding one. By the time his circle was a hundred yards across, dusk was coming on, and he could hear the soft buzzing of the nighthawks in the darkening sky.

The third day was Saturday. His paper route, a local weekly, took up the entire morning. He carried a copy of William Beebe's *Half Mile Down* to read as he walked from house to house. From eight in the morning until noon he drifted weightlessly and soundlessly in the bathysphere through a dark undersea world, occasionally tripping over privet hedges and wandering up driveways to retrieve newspapers that went wide of their mark.

"Harrington!" Mrs. Kraus brayed at him from her porch. "Look where you're going! Young Harrington! Get your feet out of my gladiolas!" He flushed, mumbled, "Sorry," got back onto the sidewalk, and a few moments later was back in the bathysphere, on the trail of rainbow gars and pallid sailfins.

He was going to start hunting for the den again after lunch, but he was too late. As he was walking up the long curving driveway toward the house, his empty newspaper bag over his shoulder and his nose still deep in William Beebe, he heard the shotgun again, two thumps this time. He dropped the Beebe in the driveway and started running up the hill, the canvas bag flapping against his thighs. As he neared the house, he saw Karman walking out into the field to the west, still carrying the gun. Mike cut across the fallow field to intercept him, still moving at a run. Near the brush at the edge of the field, Karman stopped and seemed to be peering about. Mike, breathing hard, caught up with him there. "God damn you!" he yelled. The man turned, stared at him. "It was a fox!" Mike yelled again. "It wasn't the hawks!"

The man turned away from him, back toward the brush. "Not dead," he said. Mike saw the hawk then. It was right at the edge of the brush, down on the ground. One wing hung limply to the earth, but the bird was staring at them defiantly, its beak open, clearly prepared to stand its ground.

Karman looked pained. He ran his tongue along his lips. He raised the old double barrel toward his shoulder.

"No," Mike said, and pushed the gun to the side. The man turned toward him again, shaking his head and looking miserable. "Not let suffer," he said, his voice almost

65

pleading. He raised the gun again, brought it to bear. Mike didn't say anything this time. Instead, he jumped out in front of the gun and ran toward the hawk, then spun around. Karman stared at him, mouth open, down the barrel of the shotgun. "Go ahead and shoot, you . . ." He stopped for a moment, wondered what Kermit Roosevelt might have said. "You churl," he said. Slowly Karman lowered the gun. His mouth hung open. His shoulders slumped.

Mike turned back toward the hawk, which watched him from a few feet away. Now what do I do? he wondered. He approached the bird carefully. It had been dead silent up till now, but suddenly it began to hiss like a snake. It rocked back on its tail and one good wing and raised one of its talons. "Oh, boy," Mike said out loud. Facing down Karman had been one thing, but the hawk, which aside from its trailing wing appeared quite uninjured, was obviously formidable and obviously ready to fight.

"Easy now," Mike said softly, trying to sooth it with his voice, and moving around to the side. The hawk's head swiveled to follow him, and when he reached out tentatively, it hissed again and bounded toward him. He drew back, startled. The bird stood its ground and looked slowly back and forth from him to Karman.

Mike moved up again. The hawk bounced forward to confront him. Feathers puffed out in aggression, it looked the size of an eagle.

"The bag," Karman said suddenly. Mike stared at him. The man pointed. "Your bag," he said again. He was pointing at Mike's newspaper bag. "I help you. I make him watch me. You put bag from in back."

Karman put the shotgun on the ground. He stood in a crouch and began flapping his arms like wings and hopping about and clucking like a chicken. The hawk riveted its Medusa gaze on the man, hopped about to face him. "The bag," Karman said, and squawked again, and flapped his arms. Mike, finally reacting, took the canvas bag from his shoulder, hesitated for a moment, then lunged forward and popped the mouth of it down over the redtail.

The bag seemed to explode underneath him, but he managed to get it turned over with the hawk more or less inside, and twisted the carrying strap to close the mouth. Mike knelt beside it, his breath coming fast.

Karman stood looking down at him, shaking his head.

"Thanks," Mike said.

"Is all right," the man said. "I did not like shoot anyway. But now what you do with him?"

Mike looked down at the erupting canvas. A huge yellow talon that looked as if it could tear an arm off was sticking out the top of the bag.

"I don't know," he said.

The old woodshed behind the house was a good-sized out-building containing two rooms. In the smaller front room Mike kept half a dozen cages containing some snakes, a box turtle, and a collared lizard, but the larger back room was empty except for a few garden tools. In that back room, he dumped the hawk out of the sack. It stood on the floor in front of him, talons gripping into the old wood, in an attitude of total defiance. Beak agape, it stretched its head toward him and hissed like a viper. It looked ludicrous stretched out that way, but menacing at the same time. Mike took a step backward. "Now what do I do with you?" he said aloud.

He had a vague idea. The previous spring he'd caught a young sparrow hawk, a pretty miniature falcon, just out of the nest and still unable to fly properly. The bird was too small to capture any wild game large than a mouse or a sparrow, but Mike dug up a musty old falconry book in the library and studied the principles of training a hawk. The book was written in an archaic language that fascinated him; he read of tiercels and haggards and birds of passage, of jesses and bewits and brails and varvels, of bating and coping and bowsing. But he had little opportunity to put his new knowledge into practice, for the sparrow hawk escaped a few days after he'd caught it.

The redtail was not a nestling like the sparrow hawk, but a passage hawk—a mature, experienced bird captured from the wild. There were several ways to train a passager, but the book had said that the best way was a technique called "waking"—the best, anyway, if the falconer could stand it.

The hawk hissed again. "Now take it easy," Mike said. "You just stay here and be quiet. It's going to be a long night." Then he backed out and closed the door after him.

Down at the house he gathered the things he'd need. He got a pair of his mother's gardening gloves, then, remembering the look of those huge talons, he got another pair of his father's leather work gloves as well. He had no leather to make proper jesses, so he took the rawhide thongs from his hiking boots. He found a couple of candles in the sideboard, got some books from his room, and some old stockings from his mother's ragbag to bind up the injured wing. He was raiding the icebox when his mother found him. "You'll spoil your dinner," she said.

"It's not for me." He rooted around in the Frigidaire. "It's for the hawk."

"The what?"

"Old man Karman wounded one, and I got it before he killed it. *Buteo jamaicensis,* the eastern red-tailed hawk."

"Lord help us," his mother said. "What next?"

"I won't be home tonight," Mike said. "I've got to spend tonight in the woodshed."

"You're going to spend the *night* in the *woodshed*?"

"I have to stay with the hawk. Maybe tomorrow night and the next night too. That's how you tame them down. You keep them awake, don't let them sleep for two or three days, and finally they get so sleepy they don't hate you anymore, all they want to do is sleep."

"Young man," she said, "you'll catch your death out there."

"No," Mike said. "I'll take a blanket, the nights are pretty warm now anyhow."

"That's your father's kidneys," she said.

"It's the only thing I can find in here he'd eat," Mike said. "Hawks don't eat Cheerios, you know. After this, I'll get food for him out of my paper money and get some starlings with my BB gun, but I really need some food for him now, Mom."

She sighed. "I think your father is going to want to see you when he gets home," she said.

Arms laden, Mike went back up to the woodshed. Inside, the hawk was nowhere to be seen. Mike dropped his gear, looked around the room. He couldn't have got out, he thought. Could Andy have come up here and opened the door while I was gone?

Then, down in the corner under the workbench, he saw

70

a gleaming eye regarding him balefully. He dropped to his hands and knees. "Come on out of there," he said. "That's no place for a hawk." The bird was pressed back into the corner, its feathers a tangle of cobwebs. It opened its beak and hissed. Its wide, wild eyes were full of murder. "Boy, you sure do hate me," Mike said.

Mike got up from the floor, began to prepare himself. The job ahead of him, he knew, was going to be terribly difficult. The bird had to be tamed, but its spirit could not be broken. The normal technique of animal training, of reward and punishment, was useless against its intractable wildness. Punishment would only drive it into rage. The only solution was infinite, monolithic patience.

He knew that he had to get his makeshift jesses, the leather thongs, tied to the bird's feet so that it could not get away from him and then convince it, somehow, to perch on his fist. He tied loops in the ends of the thongs so that they'd be ready, put them in his teeth, then put on both pairs of gloves, Down on all fours, he approached the bird. "Come on, baby," he mumbled around the leather in his teeth, but the hawk scuttled crabwise across the floor to the other corner, dragging its wing. Mike crawled after it, mumbling what he hoped were soothing and reassuring sounds. He moved very slowly, inching across the floor. When he was three feet away, the redtail roused, puffing out its feathers till it seemed double its size. Then it came at him, half flying, half hopping, and Mike saw only the talons and the strong hooked beak, and he recoiled so sharply that he went over backward. He lay there on the floor and looked at the hawk, which stood now against the wall and glared at him. Mike's heart was pounding. This bird was nothing like the sparrow hawk—

its talons were big enough to be dangerous. "Okay," he said. "Maybe the jesses can wait for a while. Maybe we better just get used to each other first."

Cautiously, he picked himself up, got a rickety stool from the front room, and put it in the corner opposite the hawk. For the next hour he and the bird stared at each other. The bird did not attack him, but the fury never left its eyes—it looked as if it wanted to kill him. "Attila," he said. "Attila the Hun. The Scourge of God. That name suits your personality."

The hawk glared.

"Maybe I shouldn't look at you," Mike said aloud. In the world of animals, he knew, a fixed gaze was the mark of a predator contemplating an attack, and the hawk might feel challenged by his stare. So, for a while he gazed at the ceiling, at the floor, at corners of the room. The technique seemed to improve the hawk's disposition somewhat, but the minute he turned his eyes full on it again, the redtail roused and seemed ready to commit mayhem. So, for another hour he observed it with furtive sidelong glances while the hawk stared at him.

He tried again, crawling slowly up to the hawk without looking at it. To his surprise, this time it remained reasonably calm, and moving with infinite slowness, he was able to attach the jesses to its feet. Now to get it on his fist. He remembered reading that the way to get a hawk on the fist was to press the glove against the back of its legs—the bird would step back instinctively. While the hawk watched his every movement, he looped the ends of the jesses around his fingers, then moved his gloved hand around and behind the bird, nudging it slightly.

Primly, precisely, the hawk stepped back, and there it

stood on his gloved hand, gripping firmly with its talons. "Aren't you a good bird?" Mike murmured.

Holding his breath, Mike rose slowly from the floor until he stood erect. The bird seemed right at home and unruffled. "Aren't you a lovely Scourge of God," Mike murmured. "This won't be so bad after all."

Then the hawk bated off, simply dove headlong off his fist in a wild attempt to fly, and wound up spinning head downward from the jesses, buffeting his thighs with its one good wing. Mike got his other hand under the hawk and tilted it back up onto his fist. It bated again. He picked it up. It bated again. He picked it up. It bated.

After the fifteenth bate, Mike was trembling. The hawk's wild rage was frightening. It seemed as if the bird was never going to settle down, that it would break its own wings with its wild flailings or slice pieces from him with its talons. He picked it up once more. The hawk bated. "Oh, come on," Mike pleaded, his voice shaky.

Finally, the hawk sat momentarily on his fist, panting with exertion and glaring at him. "Thank God," Mike whispered. His legs were trembling, vibrating like a sewing machine.

He had just begun to relax when the woodshed door swung open, and the hawk bated wildly. His father stood in the doorway staring at him; the hawk hung upside down from his fist, thrashing.

"What in God's name are you doing?" Mr. Harrington said.

"Shut the door," Mike pleaded. "The bright light gets him excited." He tried to get the redtail back up on his fist again, but it was hopeless. The bird was in a fury. It lunged off the glove so hard the jesses slipped from Mike's fingers, and the hawk pitched onto the floor and scuttled into a corner and began to hiss.

"Jesus H. Christ," his father said.

"I'm training him," Mike said.

"Training him? It looks like you're killing him or he's killing you, or maybe both."

"You just upset him coming in like that, he doesn't like strangers."

"Doesn't like strangers? He doesn't like *anybody*. I want you to let that damn bird go back where he belongs. You've got enough crazy pets around this place, and I see no good reason for you to torture that bird by penning him up in this shed."

"I can't let him go now," Mike said. "His wing is hurt. Old Karman got him with a shotgun. A fox would get him right off, or he'd starve."

His father sighed in exasperation. "You've always got an answer," he said. "Now what's this your mother tells me about you staying out here all night?"

"That's how you tame him. You stay awake with him for a couple of nights till he gets used to you."

"You mean you're not going to sleep for the next two nights?"

"It's not hard," Mike said. "Corcoran and I stayed awake for sixty-five hours a couple of months ago, just for an experiment."

The man shook his head. "Maybe some day I'll understand," he said. "But I doubt it. Sometimes I'd just settle for a plain, ordinary juvenile delinquent." Still shaking his head, he turned and went out the door.

When he was gone, Mike turned back to the hawk, which remained crouched under the workbench. "O.K.," he said. "Back to work."

74

An hour later he had got the hawk back on his fist again and had bound the trailing wing against its body with an old stocking. He offered it a piece of kidney now. The bird turned its head away. Mike began to stroke its feet with the bit of meat. Eventually, the hawk turned back. Mike offered it the kidney. The hawk snapped it up in its bill, flicked it to the floor. "Come on, I'm not trying to poison you," Mike crooned. He picked up the kidney. "It's good," he said. "Yum, yum, Attila. Here." The bird flicked it to the floor. He picked it up, offered it. The bird flicked it to the floor.

After refusing the kidney a dozen times, at the next proffering the hawk hissed and bated. Mike looked down at the spinning bundle of feathers, feeling anger rising up in him. He clenched his teeth and closed his eyes, stood stock still for a long time. Finally, he opened his eyes and looked down at the redtail. "Okay, so we start again," he said.

He had got the hawk to eat two small bits of kidney by the time his mother brought a tray of food out to him. She didn't come in; she opened the door and peered through it, but the disturbance precipitated another half hour of frenzied bating, and his own food was cold by the time he got to eat it, standing at the workbench and forking it down with one hand while holding the hawk with the other.

"By careful stalking, they got within thirty yards of the bull," Mike said softly to the hawk. "Kermit put both barrels of his heavy double .450 into the tusker's head, but without even staggering him; and as he walked off, Tarleton also fired both barrels into him, with no more effect; then, as he slowly turned, Kermit killed him with a shot in the brain from the .405 Winchester."

75

Mike sat at the workbench, resting his forearm against it to support the weight of the hawk. He had wrapped the blanket around his shoulders to cut the late night chill, and he read from the thick book by the flickering light of a candle. "They followed the herd again," he read to the hawk, "and Kermit got some photos which, as far as I know, are better than any that have ever before been taken of a wild elephant. He took them close up, at imminent risk of a charge."

Mike looked up from the book, glanced sidelong at the hawk, which was wide-awake and watching him carefully. "Do you know who I'd like to be, Attila, if I could be anybody?" he asked the hawk. "Kermit Roosevelt," he said. Kermit had been just about to enter Harvard, only a few years older than Mike himself, when he had gone off to Africa with his father to collect specimens of game for the Smithsonian Institution. Kermit had been rich with a famous father, he rode superbly and had been an intrepid hunter and wildlife photographer. "And here am I in this old woodshed," Mike sighed. "And my father is never going to take me to Africa." He stroked the bird's back feathers gently; the hawk permitted this. "Anyway," Mike said, "I'll bet Kermit never had a nice hawk like you."

The hawk bated.

The first gray light of dawn seeped around the edges of the shutters, the song sparrows were buzzing and trilling behind the house, and from back in the woods a catbird went through a virtuoso concert, sounding like half a dozen different birds at once. Mike walked slowly in a circle, carrying the hawk on one hand, the book in the other. "Shot by K. R.," he read in a weary monotone.

"Lion, 8. Leopard, 3. Cheetah, 7. Hyena, 4. Elephant, 3. Square-mouthed rhinoceros, 4."

His back was stiff. His shoulder ached from carrying the hawk. His legs felt numb. "Thomson's gazelle, 9," he told the hawk. "Gerunuk, 2. Klipspringer, 3. Oribi, 8. Duiker, 2. Steinbuck, 2. Dikdik, 1." He went over to the workbench, put the book down, rested his hawk arm on the bench. With his free hand he rubbed his eyes. They felt scratchy. He wanted sleep more than anything he could think of. He looked sidelong at the hawk. It stared at him, alert. Mike sighed, picked up the book, began to walk again, round and round in circles.

"Flamingo, 4. Whale-headed stork, 1, on wing. Marabou, 1. Guinea fowl, 5 . . ."

The second day was a repeat of the first. Roused by the daylight coming in around the shutters, the hawk grew wild and intractable. It hissed. It threw pieces of kidney on the floor. It bated when it heard the Cadillac start up, bated when his little brother came up to try to see what was going on, went into a frenzy when it sensed the dog snuffling around outside the shed, bated when it heard the Cadillac return.

Early in the afternoon Mike left the hawk in the shed and walked around outside in the sunlight. His legs felt shaky. Down at the house his mother stuffed him with lunch and tried to talk him into taking a nap. "I can't," he said. "I'm not going to give up now." He called Corcoran on the phone, told him about the hawk. "He's crazy," Mike said. "He's been up all night and I thought I really had him gentled down, and now he wants to kill me again."

"Can I help?" Corcoran asked.

"I don't think so. Anything new seems to upset him."

"Courage, Mole," Corcoran said. "Hang in there."

Mike rode his bicycle down to the school library and found the old falconry book, *The Art and Practice of Hawking,* and took it back to the woodshed with him. When he got there, he found the hawk, its jesses caught in a crack, hanging head down from the workbench and beating its good wing against the floor. He got it back on his fist, propped the book on the workbench, and began to read.

The falconer's tone of voice, warned the book, was very important, "for the harsh tones of an angry or peevish man must give any intelligent animal a bad notion of his character." The falconer must not exhibit petulance or make rough or sudden movements—if a gnat bothered him, he was not to swat it. The falconer should not expose a new hawk to women, which were apt to upset it, to children, which would upset it even more, nor to dogs, which would upset it most of all.

The book advised that he be careful when stepping over a stile, because hawks did not like being lowered suddenly, and that he learn to hold his hand absolutely steady even when in a joggling dogcart, so as not to displease the bird by bouncing it about. He was to be sure, when passing through a doorway, that he didn't allow the bird's tail to brush against the door, and was to be especially careful not to get near anyone wearing a stiff-brimmed hat. Once the hawk was partly trained, it could be gradually introduced to such loathesome elements of society as women and children, so long as they did not stare impudently at the bird, for that would annoy it. Finally, the bird could be accustomed slowly to noise and commotion. A very good place to do this, the book said, was the billiard room.

Mike looked up at the hawk, which was staring at him. "The billiard room?" he said. "Attila, I'm not sure we're going to make it."

For the rest of the afternoon Mike read aloud to the bird, first from *The Art and Practice of Hawking* and then from Rudyard Kipling. He intoned passages from *The Light that Failed.* Emotion burring his voice, he read his favorite poem, "Great-Heart," which Kipling had written on the death of Theodore Roosevelt.

Mike's mother brought his dinner to the shed. His father did not come to see him.

"There was no sound from behind," his voice said to the hawk, "except a faint, plaintive whine from one of the dogs, which I imagined was in reply to a touch from Ninnis' whip. I remember addressing myself to George, the laziest dog in my own team, saying, 'You will be getting a little of that, too, George, if you are not careful.' "

His voice sounded disembodied, as if someone else were reading. By the light of the candle he leaned over the book, Mawson's journal of antarctic exploration. "When I next looked back, it was in response to the anxious gaze of Mertz, who had turned around and halted in his tracks. Behind me, nothing met the eye but my own sledge tracks running back in the distance. Where were Ninnis and his sledge?"

Outside, the cicadas had long since been silenced by the after-midnight chill. In the shed it was totally silent. The hawk, its feathers fluffed out against the cold, sat on his fist, its eye glittering in the flickering light of the candle. The voice began again. "When comrades tramp the road to anywhere through a lonely blizzard-ridden land in hunger, want and weariness, the interests, ties and fates of each are interwoven in a wondrous fabric of friendship and affection. The shock of Ninnis' death struck home and deeply stirred us. He was a fine fellow and a born soldier." Mike looked at the photograph in the old book, in the candlelight saw the handsome young man with level eyes, ramrod straight in his smart uniform. "Lieutenant B.E.S. Ninnis," he told the hawk, a slight catch in his voice. "Royal Fusiliers."

He read on, absorbed, trying to keep his voice soothing and steady in spite of the drama. When Ninnis' sledge plunged into the crevasse, the strongest dogs, Basilisk, Ginger Bitch and Shackleton, had perished, and most of the food was gone. But Mawson and Mertz pressed on, through bone-numbing cold. They grew weaker day by day. "At 2:00 A.M. on the 17th we had only covered eleven miles when we stopped to camp. Then Mertz shot and cut up Johnson while I prepared the supper. Johnson had always been a faithful, hardworking and willing beast, with rather droll ways of his own, and we were sorry that his end should come so soon. He could never be accused of being a handsome dog, in fact he was generally disreputable and lazy.

"The paws took longest of all to cook," he read to the hawk, "but, treated to lengthy stewing, they became quite digestible."

"Holy cow," Mike said softly. He put his arm across the book, put his head down on it. "I'll just rest my eyes for a minute," he told the hawk.

It felt wonderful to have his eyes closed, like slipping into a warm sea. He imagined Ninnis among the broken bodies of his dogs, 150 feet down in the blue ice of the crevasse. Poor old Ninnis, he thought. Another name in his pantheon of heroes. Kermit. Byrd, alone at advance base with his deadly fume-producing stove and the frost creeping daily higher up the walls. Raymond L. Ditmars, slogging through the swamps of Trinidad in search of rare toads. William Beebe in the depths of the sea. Carl Akeley, facing the charge of an enraged bull elephant to collect specimens for the American Museum. Audubon on his great horse Barro, ranging the wilderness in his quest for birds. Lieutenant M. R. Harrington, Royal Fusiliers, he thought. Soldier, naturalist, explorer.

The wind was picking up. Ahead, it whipped the snow through the frozen furrows of sastrugi, and he could feel it cut like a knife through his heavy parka. He stopped, squinting at the low sun that reflected off the endless fields of ice. It had grown colder. Sixty below now, he judged. He looked down at Basilisk, the great full-blooded timber wolf. The wolf returned his look from intelligent eyes. "It's just the two of us now," he said. "Two against the cold." The wolf pressed its head against his thigh. "We must push on," he said. Then, leaning into the wind, squinting his frost-rimed eyes against the driving particles of snow, he trudged deliberately forward, ever southward toward the Pole. . . .

The President leaned toward him across the huge polished desk. "Bully," Great-Heart said, his bushy mustache aquiver. "Bully, my lad. I am personally recommending you for the gold medal of the National Geographic Society and for election to the Explorer's Club. You have brought great honor to your country."

"I only tried to do my best, sir," he said modestly.

*"This evening you must report here to the White House
and tell Kermit and me all about it over sherry."*

*"Thank you very much, sir," he replied, and rose to
leave.*

*"And by the way, lad," the President said. "I'm sorry
about the dog. It must have been most difficult toward
the end."*

*"Yes," he said, "though the paws were quite digestible
when stewed."*

*"I know how you must feel," the President said sym-
pathetically.*

"There'll never be another like Basilisk, sir," he said.

Mike jerked bolt upright at the bench, looked around
in bewilderment. Where was the hawk?

He saw it then, down at the far end of the bench in the
corner, its feathers puffed out, its eyes watching him. "I
guess I dozed off," he said sheepishly. He stood up,
rubbed his eyes, stretched the stiffened muscles of his
back. He walked outside the woodshed, peed in the dew-
wet grass. Down below, the house was dark. Faint in the
distance he could hear a big truck groaning through its
gears up Blair Hill, a mile and a half away. Overhead the
stars were crisp in the sky. His eye found the Dipper, followed the imaginary line out to Polaris, the star of explor-
ers.

After a while he went back in again, took the hawk on
his fist, and began to walk around and around in circles.
He wanted very much to go down to the house and get
into his bed and sleep until the next afternoon. But the
falconry book had warned against those amateurs who
tried to train hawks without waking. Above all else, the

book said, the falconer must be in love with his hawk; he must be willing to accept the ordeal of training it.

At dawn the bird began to bate again. "Please," Mike pleaded, his voice unsteady. "Please stop." But the fury went on for an hour, before the redtail calmed down. His legs, by now, ached clear to the thighs.

Outside, birds began to sing. Beams of sunlight filtered in around the edges of the shutters. The hawk shifted its grip on his glove. Mike looked down at it. It looked up at him. Its good wing began to droop. Then, slowly, the lids rolled up over its great eyes. There, on his gloved fist, it slept as if that were the only perch it had ever known.

Mike sat in his hawk mews—he had rechristened the woodshed—talking softly to Attila, who glared at him furiously. "You'd like to tear me limb from limb, wouldn't you?" Mike crooned. "You'd like to pluck my heart out and have it for breakfast. You old devil, you. You lovely old devil." The bird shifted its yellow feet, hunched its shoulders. "Now don't bate," Mike said, and after a moment the bird relaxed.

So far the hawk had responded well to his training, and though it still flew into fits of rage, it sometimes tolerated him now as a source of food and perhaps even as company. He shot starlings and English sparrows for it with his air rifle, carried it about on his fist for hours, and gave it the sun every day, leashed to its bow perch in front of the shed.

For guidance Mike referred frequently to *The Art and Practice of Hawking*, which gave him abundant advice, not all of it easy to follow or even to understand. The book advised him that he should develop the touch of an organist and the hands of a sculptor, otherwise his hawk might get disgusted with him. The hawk could be counted upon to dislike bathing before 11:00 A.M. and getting rained on a lot—in bad weather, the falconer should carry an umbrella, not for himself but for his bird. The bird needed to be protected from such maladies as croaks, cramps, catarrh, frounce, megrim and apoplexy, and the falconer should certainly not let his hawk become afflicted with a snurt. If the bird got mites, its beak was to be bathed in a mixture of water, tobacco, and brandy; in case of fever its feet were to be washed in water distilled from lettuce; if a wing drooped, the hawk was to be held over a pot of steaming wine. To keep the hawk in good condition, the falconer might occasionally dose it with a nostrum of mummy, mogemort, indorum, kabalorum and polipodic, all mixed together and served up in a hen's gut.

Without benefit of hen's gut, polipodic, or steaming wine, the redtail's injured wing had mended rapidly. Two days before, Mike had removed the makeshift sling, and to his delight the hawk immediately began to flex the great pinion, fanning the air with power. Next week, Mike would begin training the bird for the hunt.

While at the library, Mike had asked the librarian if there were any poems about hawks and had brought some books home with him. He picked one up from the bench

85

now and riffled through it. "Here, you'll like this one," he said to the hawk. "It's about a wounded redtail, just like you." He began reading aloud from the Jeffers:

> . . . the great redtail
> Had nothing left but unable misery
> From the bone too shattered for mending,
>   the wing that trailed under his talons
>   when he moved.
> We had fed him six weeks, I gave him freedom,
> He wandered over the foreland hill and
>   returned in the evening, asking for death,
> Not like a beggar, still eyed with the old
> Implacable arrogance.

Mike stopped, looked at the hawk. "That's you," he said to the redtail. "Implacable arrogance—that's you, all right."

He started to read on, but paused when he heard the deep, foggy sound of a conch shell blowing. Once, twice, a third time, each note so deep in tone that it gave him a shiver in his bones. "The call of the Toad," he told the hawk. "Now don't bate while I'm gone." He went into the front room of the shed, took his own conch from its nail, went outside and blew two long, lip-stinging blasts. He checked the hawk, then headed on up the hill toward the pond.

In the woods he moved slowly, watching where he placed his feet, trying to avoid stepping on twigs that would give away his position. As he walked, he moved his head in a slow circle, looking left and right, then up, then down, then behind him, in the time-honored method of great hunters and naturalists. As he neared the pond, he moved even more stealthily. It was his ambition to move

86

imperceptibly as a tree growing, so that he could materialize a foot away from Corcoran without his friend's being aware of him, at which moment he would quote casually the Nilghai's great line, "There'll be trouble in the Balkans in the spring"—and scare Corcoran right out of his skin.

Corcoran spotted him when he was fifty feet away, picked up his conch from the log where he was sitting, and made a farting sound into it. Then he raised his hand, palm forward, in greeting. "Brave Mole."

The two boys sat side by side on the log. Corcoran dug in the leaves for the cache of grapevines, and they lit up and sat looking out over the water. "How's the hawk?" Corcoran asked.

"The training's going well. It's a good thing, because everything else around here is going bellyup."

"The bulldozer, you mean?"

Mike nodded, and Corcoran said, "You know, Dad has been talking about that, about the building boom that's starting up. You know, he's so excited now because he thinks he's going to make some money on that property he's got out on Center Road, but I never thought about it around here. You know, it's not so bad for me because I have the chemistry and all, but that's pretty rough on a biologist."

"Even my trees," Mike said. "My Moses Cleaveland trees. I've got to do something."

"What?"

"I don't know. I haven't been able to figure it out yet."

"I'll try to think, too," Corcoran said. "Meantime, Mole, cheer up. I've got a plan."

"What?"

"There's that summer dance at school tonight."

"Oh, yeah, I'd forgot."

"Dad went to Indianapolis on a business trip today. Took the train. Mom is spending the night at my aunt's. You know what that means?"

"Wheels?"

"Wheels. The pater's Ford V-8 convertible."

"You know, you're going to get caught with that phony driver's license one of these days."

"I spent three days working on that license in the school photo lab," Corcoran said. "It's a masterpiece. I'm not going to get caught. I'm big enough to pass for sixteen. Just so I don't speed or run a stoplight. You want to come along?"

"Oh, I thought I might collect tonight. Not much chance left for any *Pseudacris.*"

Corcoran blew out a puff of acrid grapevine smoke. "You know, Mole, you ought to learn to dance."

"Nuts," Mike said.

"I mean it. Come on along. With the car, we can get something tonight."

"Oh, come on," Mike said angrily. The thing was, Corcoran probably *would* get something.

"O.K. There I'll be with a handful of Marilyn Bishop's mammaries—two handsful, she's so big. And there you'll be with a handful of some vile amphibian."

Mike didn't say anything. He thought about Angeline Karman's breasts.

Corcoran said, "You know, Mike, I'm going to get a stone-ache again tonight." He laughed. "The thing I don't understand is, if people always get a stone-ache, why do they do it all the time?" He stubbed out his grapevine in the moist earth. "But I want to do it anyway."

88

"I'll go," Mike said.

"Aha!"

"Okay, I'll go." Mike stood up.

Corcoran raised his hand, palm forward. "I will meet you when the setting sun sinks behind Karman's chicken coop," he said.

"When the big hand is at twelve and the little hand is at seven."

"Till this evening, then, my good Mole."

"Farewell, Toad."

In his checked wool sport coat and his father's red-and-blue striped tie with his shoes shined carefully to cover the scuff marks, and his belt buckled on the side, he stood in a knot of boys under the basketball backboard in the gymnasium, while the dancing couples bounced and gyrated on the dance-waxed floor. Out there Corcoran, in his double-breasted sky-blue suit with the pegged pants, his pink wide-collared shirt, and Windsor-knotted tie, was dancing with Marilyn Bishop to the Detroit Polka, as played on record by Frankie Yankovic and his Yanks. Corcoran danced very well and so did Marilyn. Spinning in the polka steps, her blond hair swirled and her flared dress flew above her knees. She wore a pink angora sweater, and her big breasts bobbled around under it so that Mike couldn't take his eyes off them.

"Wouldn't you like some of that, Brains?"

Mike looked around. Eddie Valeski stood there, looking neat in his drapes and letter sweater. Eddie was fullback on the freshman football team, a neckless fellow with a flat mat of blond hair on top of a square head. He acted dumb, aping the senior high athletes, but he really wasn't. He even read books he didn't have to read. Mike liked him.

"Some tits," Mike said. It seemed the right word.

"Yeah, boy, that's eatin' stuff." He punched Mike in the shoulder—not hard, but friendly. "Brains," he said, "you ever get any? A piece of ass?"

"No, I never did."

"Old lady five-fingers, huh?"

Mike flushed. "Oh, knock it off, Eddie," he said sharply.

Valeski laughed. "Okay, Brains," he said. "I wouldn't want you to get mad and beat me up." His expression grew serious. "You know, my sister can dance the polka, my brother can dance the polka. My mother and father invented the polka. I'm the only Valeski that can't do the polka."

"Well," Mike said, "neither can I."

"It's okay for you, Brains," Valeski said. "You aren't a football player. You aren't a Polack. You ever hear of a Polack football player who can't dance the polka? I'm a disgrace to my race."

"Why don't you get your sister to teach you?"

"I've tried—I just can't seem to learn. Whenever I try to learn one of those steps, it's like I'm charging off tackle. One time I knocked my sister down, and that ended that. You know, I've never had a piece of ass either, and I just know I could get one if I could only learn to dance. Look at them out there. Those girls got to be getting excited jumping around like that. I'm excited just watching. I'll bet your buddy Corcoran is going to get a little tonight. The polka—that's what stands between me and carnal knowledge."

90

Valeski drifted away, morose and heavy-shouldered. After a while, Mike began to drift, too, joining the squad of boys who ceaselessly patrolled the edges of the dance floor. Like the others, he never asked anyone to dance, but he felt less conspicuous than if standing in one place and more purposeful, like a hunter simply biding his time while seeking appropriate game. After a dance, even without actually having got out onto the floor with a girl, he usually felt exhausted from all the miles he'd clocked.

He looked at girls. The big spinning mirror ball suspended from the gymnasium ceiling picked little colored highlights on their clothes. Angora sweaters were popular that year, and Mike studied them. "You're getting as bad as old Toad," he told himself. "You're going to go crazy if you don't quit thinking about breasts all the time." He saw Angeline, dancing rather primly with another girl from their class. She was wearing a green skirt and white blouse and ballerina shoes and nylon stockings, and her legs looked smooth as sculpture. He'd never seen Angeline wearing anything but bobby socks before and looking at her legs made him feel steamy.

Between dances, Corcoran found him posted under the backboard again. "How are you doing, Mole?" he said. The jacket of his suit was covered with pink fuzz from rubbing against Marilyn Bishop's angora-pelted breasts. He looked red in the face and excited.

"I'm doing okay."

"Baloney. I haven't seen you dancing all night."

"You know I can't do the polka, and that's all they ever play. I danced when they played 'Laura.' With Carol Galaba."

"Forget her, Mole. You'll never get any of that. She

91

goes out with seniors. She was just being nice to you for getting her through English. How about Angeline Karman? Have you danced with the fair Angeline?"

"No, dammit, I haven't danced with the fair Angeline, what's it to you?"

"Well, there she is over there, Mike, and she hasn't been dancing much tonight. She's just waiting."

"Not for me."

"Look, Mike, you're smart, but you're really stupid. Even if she's not madly in love with you, there she is, she doesn't want to stand around and dance with other girls all night. You are the vice president of the freshman class, and you didn't win that just with votes from the boys. You should have a little more confidence. Now go over and recite her a little Keats or Shelley or something, sweep her off her feet. After the dance we can take her and Marilyn home and have some fun."

"Okay," Mike said. "Just lay off, I'll ask her to dance next time there's a slow one."

"There's a slow one starting now," Corcoran said. "Forward, Child of the Pit!"

Mike checked the knot in his tie, checked his fly, brushed his hair back. "O.K.," he said wryly. "The hunter stalks his prey."

"You always hurt the one you love," sang the Mills Brothers. Angeline's dark hair brushed against his face, and he felt as if he were sinking down into a swimming pool full of perfume. Against his chest he could feel her breasts, her brassiere anyway. He wanted to hold her closer, but he thought she might pull back, and besides, if they danced any closer, she would know how excited he was. What did other guys do? he wondered. Maybe they didn't get excited. Maybe the girls didn't care.

"I think this music is so lovely," Angeline said into his ear.

"Amplification's not so hot," Mike said. "Too much impedence."

"When I hear music like this, I sort of feel things welling up inside me."

Mike tilted his head back to look at her. That sounded like a line out of one of her movie magazines. He realized that she'd changed her hair, parting it a bit to the side now and letting it tumble down, which made her look more than ever like Elizabeth Taylor, except her nose was too small and her eyes were dark brown, almost black.

"Does music ever make you feel you want to cry?" Angeline said.

"Ah, I guess so."

"You're a very sensitive person," Angeline said. "I think that's so important. You know, there are a lot of times I feel like crying. Like when I walk in the rain. I love to walk in the rain."

"Really?" Suddenly, before he'd expected it, the music ended. He dropped Angeline's hand as if it had been a hot rock. Oh, God, he thought.

Angeline stood there. "Thank you for the dance, Mike," she said.

"Yes, well, thank you, Angeline. Ah, you want to come home with me? I mean, Corcoran's got his dad's car, we could drop you off, it's so close and everything. I mean, it's really quite convenient."

"Sure," Angeline said.

"It wouldn't be any trouble at all, I mean we won't get you home late or anything."

"It would be nice if you took me home."

Mike couldn't believe it. "Well," he said. "Well, that's fine Angeline. Well . . . that's bully."

They stopped at the Shore Drive-in for Cokes and hamburgers. When the girls went off to use the bathroom, Corcoran turned around to the back seat and said, "Listen, Mole, let's take them up to the pond."

"To the *pond*?"

"Sure. Look, we can park up there on the dirt road and neck, get a feel."

"Oh, my God," Mike said. "Come off the camel, Dickie."

"I'm serious. When we get up there, you take Angeline to see the pond. Show her the *Rana pipiens* and the *Dytiscus*. Marilyn and I will stay in the car. If we all stay together, we can't get anywhere."

"Jeez, they're not going to go to the pond with us."

"Sure they are," Corcoran said. "Leave it to me."

As they started to pull out of the drive-in a few minutes later, Marilyn said, "Why don't you put the top down? I never saw anybody with a convertible who rode around in the summer with the top up."

"I thought you girls might be cold," Corcoran said.

"You're just afraid the cops will see you're too young to drive." Marilyn giggled.

"I'm not too young—I mean, I'm not afraid of the cops. I've got a license I fixed up."

"Then why are you sitting on a pillow?"

"It's just the seat's too low."

"Oh, yeah!" Marilyn laughed.

Corcoran jammed on the brakes. "Look, I don't mind having the top down as long as you girls aren't cold. That's all I'm worried about." He unlatched the top, pressed the switch that made it go back. Angeline sat primly and silently through all this, hands in her lap. Mike looked at her out of the corner of his eye. "I hope you won't be cold," he said. Actually, he hoped she'd be freezing to death, and he'd have to put his arm around her to keep her warm.

"Oh, no, I'll be fine."

"Well, just let me know if you get cold." His head smacked back against the seat as Corcoran gunned the engine, snapped the clutch, and screeched out of the drive-in, throwing gravel. The tires screamed on the asphalt, and the car fishtailed into the oncoming lane, then drifted back as Corcoran got it under control. "Lot of go in a Ford," Corcoran said, his voice pitched a little high. "Lot of guts."

They cruised along in silence, just the sound of the tires on the asphalt and the ratcheting of cicadas on the summer air. Corcoran turned off on Ridge Road. Nobody spoke. When he turned on to Elm Lane, still nobody spoke; they just cruised on in self-conscious silence.

When Corcoran turned onto the dirt road leading to the pond, Marilyn said loudly, "Where are we going?"

"Oh," Corcoran said, "we thought we'd show you the pond."

"The *pond?*"

"It's just a place we know," Corcoran said, and kept driving purposefully. When the road petered out, he braked to a stop.

"So what are we going to do here?" Marilyn said.

"I thought we'd look at the moon, actually," Corcoran said, his voice casual but firm.

"The *moon?*" Marilyn laughed.

"It's in its gibbous phase," Mike said.

"If we're going to neck," Marilyn said, "I don't know why we didn't go to Sandy Creek Park. That's where everybody goes. This place looks like it's full of *mosquitoes.*"

"They're not so bad, Marilyn," Corcoran said. "We can put the top up again."

"Oh, all right."

Mike sat dumbly, afraid to look at Angeline. Here was Marilyn gabbing away about necking, with Angeline sitting right in the car. Without looking at her, he said, "Angeline, let's go for a walk." His voice came out sounding masterful, he thought.

He got the flashlight from Corcoran's glove compartment. When they left the car, Corcoran was raising the top. "Don't you two do anything I wouldn't do," Marilyn called after them, as they started away into the dark. Mike led the way toward the pond, the girl beside him. He felt her fingers gripping his arm. Jeez, he thought, and flexed his muscle. "Mike, I can't see," she said. "Can you put on the flashlight?"

"The light just messes up your night vision," he said. "The trick of walking in the woods at night is to use the rods, not the cones. I mean, there are two kinds of light-gathering cells in the eye, and you have to use the kind called the rods, on the side of your eyeballs. So you look at things out of the side of your eyes, instead of looking straight ahead."

"You really know more than anybody, Mike."

"Maybe you'd better hold my hand," Mike said.

"All right." Her hand was cool, delicate.

Ye gods, Mike thought, we are actually holding hands. "Oops!" He stumbled over a root, almost fell.

"Oh!" Angeline gasped.

"I guess I must have looked through the cones," Mike said.

A few minutes later they reached the log. "This is where I sit when I'm collecting," Mike said. "Sort of my base camp. You want to sit down?"

"All right."

On the log they sat close, Mike still holding her hand. She didn't try to remove it. For some time they sat in silence. Mike didn't know what to do now. An idea came to him. With his free hand he groped in the leaves beneath the log, came up with the oilcloth packet. One-handed he unwrapped it, found a length of the grapevine. "Mind if I smoke?" he said casually.

"Oh, no, I didn't know you smoked. Go ahead." He disengaged the shotgun shells, lit a match on his thumbnail, took a deep puff, and blew the smoke out through his nose, which stung like crazy.

"I like the smell of your tobacco," Angeline said. "It's very masculine."

"Well, it's only a grapevine, actually," Mike said. "A little strong, but I've acquired a taste for it."

Silence. Cricket frogs chirped. The air was balmy, warm with summer, musky with the smell of the pond. After a while Mike said, "I'm sorry I had that trouble with your father about the hawk."

"Dad isn't mad," she said. "He just carries on about his chickens. He thinks you're very smart."

"Well, I'm sorry just the same." Mike wondered if he should put his arm around her. She was very close, her perfume mixing with the pond musk to make an aroma that went all the way into his brain.

"It's kind of smelly here," Angeline said.

97

"I guess I'm used to it. I come here all the time."

"You come all *alone*?"

"Corcoran comes with me sometimes. Wolf comes, but he splashes around so much he scares everything in sight."

"Wolf?"

"The dog, you know, our dog."

"I thought his name was Bozo."

"My father calls him Bozo, but I call him Wolf. I think that's a better name for a dog, don't you?"

"Ugh," Angeline said. "I think it's a *fearsome* name." They were silent for a moment, and then Angeline said, "What are all those noises?"

"You mean the ones that sound sort of like crickets? Those are the cricket frogs. The ones that sound like a plucked rubber band are green frogs. The one that sounds like a bird singing—you hear that now?—that's a toad. This is a great pond. It's got just about everything in it. I come here to collect *amphibia* and *hexapoda,* mostly. And *crustacea.* I've found eight species of salamanders here, two of toads, *americanus* and *fowleri.* Nine species of diving beetles, four of water bugs."

"All *that's* in here?"

"Sure," Mike said. "I guess you maybe think it's kind of silly for me to be so interested in natural history."

"Oh, no. You know, Elizabeth Taylor is very interested in natural history too."

"She is?"

"She has a great many pets. She has a cat named Jeepers Creepers and a horse named King Charles, that's the one she rode in *National Velvet* and the studio gave it to her, I think that was very nice of them. And a chipmunk named Nibbles. He eats cake and ice cream with hot chocolate sauce, and she's writing a book about him. I think she's such a sensitive person."

"I never knew all that," Mike said. "Say, if you'd like a chipmunk, I could probably livetrap one for you pretty easy."

"Oh, Daddy would never let me keep it. He'd be afraid it would eat up his garden."

"I suppose so," Mike said. "Would you like to see some of what's in the pond?"

"Yes," she said. She sounded interested. He got the flashlight from his coat pocket, switched it on. Midges floated in and out of the conical beam. He scanned the beam across the water at a low angle, sweeping left inch by inch, then slowly back to the right. The circle of light stopped on a pale balloon the size of a thumbnail. "That's a spring peeper," he said. "A little frog, see, his throat is blown up so he can make his noise."

He felt Angeline pull close, looking over his shoulder. Her perfume enveloped him. Oh, my God, he thought, she *is* interested.

"Now," he said, almost whispering. "As long as the light is on him, he'll stay there and keep singing. But if anything breaks the light beam, he'll dive. So, when you want to catch one, you have to keep the light straight on him and come up from behind with the net. Watch—I'll break the beam and make him disappear."

Rapidly he passed his hand back and forth through the flashlight beam.

"He did!" Angeline said. "He just disappeared."

"Sure," Mike said, and laughed. He felt good. "Let's see what else we can find." Raising the light, he pointed it down from a higher angle. "Now look there." A silver bubble sped horizontally beneath the surface of the water. "Backswimmer—you've got to watch them, they can sting worse than a hornet. Now—there along that elodea."

"I don't see . . ."

"Right in the center of the beam, see it?"

"Oh!"

"Water tiger—he's a big one. Let's see what else is . . ." The words stopped, frozen in his throat.

"What's *that*?"

"Oh, my God!" Mike whispered.

"What *is* it?"

"Shush," Mike whispered hoarsely. "Oh, and I don't have a net. Oh, Jesus H. Christ!"

"Mike, you shouldn't swear."

"Shush!" he commanded.

In the circle of light the creature lay still and glistening. Its slender body was about eight inches long. It had feathery gills, two tiny forelegs, and a small, neat head with unmoving eyes that reflected in tiny pinpoints the beam of the flashlight. It was a creature so rare that he had never hoped to see one.

"It's a siren salamander," Mike said. "It's never been recorded around here, I've just seen it in books. And I've got no net. A siren and I've got no net."

"You could always use your shirt," Angeline said, her voice a little sharp.

"Aw, he'd probably dive while I was taking it off," Mike said. He released Angeline's hand, swiveled slowly around, and lowered both feet into the water. "I'm going to try to get him," he whispered.

"Mike, your *shoes*!"

"Shush," Mike said. "Just wait, this will take a minute."

100

Slowly, inch by inch, he moved down the log, keeping the light beam nailed on the salamander's immobile head. The muck and water, cold, pressed around his ankles, then his calves.

Catching a smooth-skinned salamander floating free in the water was, he knew from experience, a matter of luck. Even if it held still till the moment he grabbed, it was so agile and slippery that it could slip from his fingers like jelly. Mike paused. His heart was banging around in his chest, and he could hear his breath coming quick. He felt frightened. This was something different. The creature that lay before him was genuinely rare, genuinely a discovery.

Very slowly, not allowing the light beam to move, he transferred the light to his left hand, freeing his right for the capture. Then he began to move forward again, ever so slowly.

He felt something now that he had never felt before, an odd sensation of being disembodied, as if watching himself from some high treetop as he moved through the pond. It was like seeing himself through the wrong end of a pair of binoculars. He felt himself grow calm, his pounding heart stilled. His body felt like an oiled machine, his motion through the water imperceptible. Now he stood above the still unmoving salamander, arm and hand rigid, poised like a heron's beak. "*Siren intermedia,*" a voice said inside his head, "you are mine." And the machine of his hand blurred down.

"*Jeez!*" Mike yelled. The salamander slithered out of his fist like a grape popped from its skin. He grabbed wildly, half caught it in the air, lost it again going away from him. Dropping the flashlight, he dove headfirst toward the still airborne creature with both hands and crashed full-face into the pond.

He came up with both hands pressed against his chest, a ball of muck and pondweed with something inside, alive and slithering. "I've got it!" he yelled. The flashlight, lying two feet under water, illuminated him with a ghostly yellow light. "I've got it."

"Mike!" Angeline shrieked.

"I can't hang onto him," Mike said. "He's so slippery. Let's get back to the car."

He took off running, stumbling through the dark woods, clutching his burden to his chest. He ran straight into a tree, stepped back with his head ringing, but he could still feel the salamander squirming between his fingers in the ball of muck. "John!" he yelled. "John, turn on the lights!" He ran on, came out of the trees and practically ran into the car's fender before he saw it. "John!" The car's windows were steamed solid. The one on the driver's side cranked down slowly. "Hey, what's wrong with you?" Corcoran's voice came out of the darkness within.

"I got a siren," Mike said, out of breath. "I got him."

"No kidding?"

"Hey, turn on some lights, I'm afraid I'm going to lose him."

Corcoran switched on the headlights and climbed out. His jacket was off, his tie pulled down, his shirttail out. His face was blotched with Marilyn's lipstick. "Hey, Mike, you're a mess." He laughed.

Mike looked down at himself in the headlight beam. His trousers were smeared with algae. His sport coat was soaked and matted with pondweed. His hands pressed the ball of muck against his white shirt. "So what," he said, "so are you."

"What's going on out there?" Marilyn's voice came from inside the car, and then she climbed out too, rearranging her clothes. She stared at Mike. "What happened to you? Where's Angeline?"

"Oh," Mike said. "Well, let me get this specimen into something and I'll go back and find her."

"Hey," Corcoran said, "are you sure you got a siren?"

"I'm sure," Mike said. "I'm really sure. What can we put it in? You got a collecting bag in the car?"

"We were going to a dance, not on a collecting trip," Corcoran said. "Say, Marilyn, could we use your purse?"

"My purse?"

"To put the salamander in," Corcoran said. "I mean just for a little while, till we get it home."

"My *purse*?" Marilyn repeated, practically shrieking. *"You're crazy!"*

"How about your undershirt?" Mike said. "You know, tie the arms to make a sack like we did when we got the ribbon snakes."

"How about *your* undershirt?" Corcoran said.

"How can I get it off without letting him go? Man, he's slippery."

"Oh, all right," Corcoran said. "Anything for science. Excuse me, Marilyn," he said. He turned his back to her, stripped off his shirt, then his undershirt, and started tying the arms in a knot.

"Hurry up," Mike said. "This guy is squirming like crazy."

"I'm hurrying as fast as I can."

"I want to go home," Marilyn said.

"Okay," Corcoran said, "dump him in."

"Let's get in front of the headlight," Mike said. "Yes, now hold it right up next to my chest, and I'll just flip this whole glob in there." Moving quickly, he spun his hands out and flipped mud, salamander, and all into the makeshift bag. "Got him!"

The two boys peered into the bag. "I'll be damned," Corcoran said softly. "It really is."

"Ugh," said Marilyn, "that's a creepy *lizard*."

"Unmistakable," Mike said. "Look at the gills. Nothing else like it."

"Take me *home*," Marilyn said.

"You going to pickle him or keep him alive?" Corcoran said.

"Keep him alive, of course," Mike said. "If we can coax him into eating. If there's one, maybe there's another. Hot damn, maybe we can get them to breed." Aware of a movement behind him, Mike turned. "Angeline!" he said.

She stood in the headlight beams like a forlorn, half-drowned sparrow. Her ballerina shoes and sculpted legs were covered with slime. Her skirt was splattered with mud. There was a scratch on her forehead, and her cheeks were wet.

"Angeline!" Marilyn cried, and ran to her. Angeline stood rigid, her hands at her sides. "It was dark," she said.

"I'm sorry, Angeline," Mike said. "I got so excited—I was coming back for you." Mike stood there clutching Corcoran's T-shirt full of gunk. He stank, he realized; his wet clothes reeked of the pond. Angeline stared at him, her large eyes moist.

"You're crazy," Marilyn said to him. "Look, her nice clothes are ruined. I want to go home, we both want to go home." She led Angeline by the hand toward the car. "You crazy creeps take us home now," she said. "We're going to sit in the back seat and you sit in front."

"Aw, Marilyn," Corcoran said. As she passed him, he tried to put his arm around her shoulder; she wheeled and hit him square in the gut with her clenched fist.

"Oof!" Corcoran gasped.

"Put your shirt on, you creep," Marilyn said. Her voice rose an octave. "And don't bring that *lizard* in this car."

"It isn't a lizard," Mike began apologetically.

"Aw, shut up, Mike," Corcoran said, clutching his belly. The girls disappeared into the back seat. Corcoran shrugged into his shirt, buttoned it, his mouth set in a line.

"Sorry, old Toad," Mike said.

"I was really making out, too," Corcoran said, stuffing his shirt into his trousers. Suddenly he looked up, grinned, began to laugh. "One more chapter in the amazing adventures of the intrepid Toad and Mole. Anything for science. Onward and upward with herpetology." He jerked his thumb toward the car. "Stick old siren in the trunk. Let's go home, Mike. Let's go have a look at the salamander."

Up the hill behind Karman's little house, Angeline's skirt and white blouse hung from the clothesline and waved gently in the breeze. Chin in his hands, Mike watched them from the window of his room. "You sure know how to mess things up, don't you?" he said to himself, and shook his head.

He got up and wandered around his room. The Nilghai squatted corpulent and immobile in his terrarium, waiting patiently for a sowbug. In their battery jars and fishbowls the backswimmers and water boatmen, the dragonfly larva and the giant water bug, swam busily or lurked among the elodea fronds according to their habits. Hannibal sculled through his battery jar, hooked jaws at the ready to seize anything that came within range. In a small aquarium the siren floated.

On the table beside the aquarium lay Mike's copy of *The Light that Failed*. When he picked it up, it fell open naturally to the passage where the Nilghai leads the men singing "The Ganges Pilot." The somber poetry suited his mood; he sat down and began to intone it aloud to the siren.

> Sounding, sounding the Ganges, floating down with the tide,
> Moor me close to Charnock, next to my nut-brown bride.
> My blessing to Kate at Fairlight—Holwell, my thanks to you;
> Steady! We steer for Heaven, through sand-drifts cold and blue.

He closed his eyes. After a moment he could hear the voices, Torpenhow and the Nilghai and Kereu the Great War Eagle and all the others, could hear the rustling of the war maps as they crowded around them making their plans, the talk of weapons and camels and generals and the Desert Column. He could see Dick Heldar there among them, blind, alone in the crowded room.

"It's nothing, really, Angeline." Inside his head he heard a voice that sounded vaguely like Ronald Colman's.

"Just an old wound from the Sudan, a nick, really, from a Fuzzy's sword."

"But your eyes, Michael, your sight."

"Nothing to trouble yourself over, really, Angeline. I

get along quite well here in my digs, and the dog, you know, is company for me." The voice laughed bitterly. "Perhaps it's just as well. They are destroying my pond, now, Angeline. I'm not sure that I could bear to—to see it. Although I do—well, I do miss my work, of course."

Her eyes had filled with tears. "I should come and take care of you, Michael."

"No. You have your own life, my dear, your own work to do. You must try your own wings. Besides—I realize that you don't love me."

"But how can I leave you like this?"

"Don't let it concern you, my dear. Actually, I've been thinking of taking a little trip. There's a spot of trouble in the Sudan again, you know, and all the boys are out there."

"But how can you go out there, as you are?" Her lip trembled.

"Oh, I shall manage somehow. I just want to smell the smoke of battle again—one last time."

"I cannot understand you, Michael," she said.

"I know," the voice said softly. "I know."

He opened his eyes. There, in front of him, the siren floated, motionless, only the gentle movement of its gills showing that it was alive. He stared at it for a long time.

The Cleveland Museum of Natural History consisted of two enormous Victorian mansions set back on a wide lawn. One of them, a vast, mustard-colored building, was the public museum—floors lined with glass cases filled with everything from the reconstructed skeleton of a coelacanth to a set of mastodon tusks twice as long as Mike was tall. Mike had spent so much time patrolling the old building's parquet floors that he knew every labyrinthine passage, every twist and turn and *cul-de-sac* between the cases. But it was the other building—a rambling, turreted structure of dark brick—that he most liked to visit. This was the working museum, the part the public did not see. It housed the library, the taxidermy and preparation shops, staff offices and laboratories, and the museum's enormous collection of study skins and preserved specimens. Here men painstakingly reconstructed the skeletons of dinosaurs and counted the scales on snakes and measured the skins of animals. This was the home of the scientists, the professionals, and when Mike visited it, he felt accepted into their world.

"Hello, Mike," Miss Morgan, the elderly receptionist, said when he came in through the heavy oak doors. "Are you going to the library today?"

Mike was the only person of his age with a pass to use the museum library, a privilege in which he took great pride. "No," he said. "Not today. I wondered if I could see Dr. Oberman." Oberman was in, he knew—he'd seen the ancient, rust-flaked, yellow Buick convertible parked in the lot out back.

Miss Morgan nodded at the brown paper bag Mike carried. "You brought him a specimen," she said.

"A salamander," Mike said.

"Well, I'm sure he'll be very pleased." Miss Morgan knew nothing about natural history, but she was very friendly. She picked up the phone. "Dr. Oberman, Joan. Dr. Oberman? Mike Harrington is here with a specimen for you. All right." She replaced the phone. "Go ahead up, Mike. Third floor, two lefts, right past the bird skins, left at the crocodile."

"I know," Mike said. Carrying his paper bag, he

climbed the broad wooden staircase, moving slowly as he always did in this building so that he had time to savor each glimpse of the world behind the museum's facade. On a landing he squeezed past a pile of dinosaur bones, encased in plaster and ricked like cordwood. Just beyond was the osteology shop and a door bearing a little sign reading, "If you feel creepy now, wait till you get inside." It was the beetle colony; inside, in darkened boxes, thousands upon thousands of dermestid beetles swarmed over the skeletons of mammals, reptiles, birds, and fish, picking them clean of every last shred of flesh with a gentle thoroughness that no scalpel or chemical could match.

He passed the enormous specimen refrigerator, a charnel house of bloody skins and animal parts, and came to the taxidermy shop where he stopped and looked in. A large high-ceilinged room, it looked more than anything like a carpentry shop—a clutter of workbenches and hand tools, paint cans and plywood and sacks of plaster of paris. Tacked to the walls were plaster casts of baboon faces and lion haunches, antelope legs and warthog heads —a Madame Tussaud's menagerie. In the middle of the room Mr. Baulkins stood on a ladder, worrying away at the head of what appeared to be the flayed body of a giant. It was Ajax. Ajax had once been an Alaska brown bear weighing 1,400 pounds and standing over nine feet tall, and his reincarnation, in wood and wire and plaster, was Mr. Baulkins' Pietà, his Sistine Chapel. At odd moments during the day, at nights, and on weekends, Mr. Baulkins had been working on Ajax for as long as Mike could remember. He had built and then destroyed as unsatisfactory two complete armatures before he achieved the looming, menacing pose that he wanted.

Baulkins looked down from the ladder. "Hello, Mike," he said. He was a small man, pale and gray, as if he had never seen the sun.

"Hi, Mr. Baulkins," Mike said. "How's old Ajax? You've sure been working on him for a long time."

"An artist can't be hurried, Mike," Baulkins said primly. "You know, this fellow here was the lord of all his domain when he was alive, and that's the way he'll look when I finish with him. Now, come on over here, tell me what you think."

Walking closer, Mike saw that a glass eye had been set into one side of Ajax's enormous head, and Baulkins was holding a matching eye against the opposite side. "The precise placement of the eyes is very important," Baulkins said. "Critical. Now, what do you think of his expression?"

"Well," Mike said, "he looks a little cross-eyed."

"Oh?" Baulkins lifted his eyebrows. He moved the eye slightly. "How about this?"

"Maybe a little higher."

"Here?"

"That looks good," Mike·said. "He looks very fierce."

"Hah!" Baulkins made a mark on the plaster head with a pencil, climbed down the ladder. He held out the glass eye to Mike. "Take a look at that. Don't drop it, though. Very best convex-concave eye, hard to get that kind since before the war."

Mike stared down at the big dark eye in his hand. It gleamed dully in the room's soft light.

"A perfect match," Baulkins said. "He'll almost be able to see out of them."

"It sure is a beauty."

Baulkins took the eye back. "I'll be ready to put his

111

skin on him in another week," Baulkins said. "You come back and see him then. By God, if he were an African mammal, he'd be fit for Akeley Hall at the American Museum." He started back up his ladder, paused. "You know," he said, "I almost hate to finish him. They'll take him over to the other building and put him on display. I want people to see my work, I like that. But I'll miss him."

"You could do another bear," Mike said.

Baulkins shook his head. "Except for Ajax, do you know what I've had to do around here for the last couple of years? Snakes. Meadow voles. Ground squirrels. Songbirds. Fish. *Fish*. What sort of work is that for a taxidermist? But who knows?" He grinned suddenly. "If this museum can ever get an expedition going now the war's over, maybe I can get something decent to do. Maybe even an elephant." The man turned and went on up the ladder.

At the door, Mike stopped and looked back. Baulkins was running his hand over the bear's enormous white shoulder and speaking to it softly: "Well, big fellow, I think we'll want to build this musculature a bit here, so it displays through the skin."

On the third floor Mike walked down a long hallway lined with steel cases and lockers containing the collection of bird study skins. The corridor was permeated with a sharp, heady smell of naptha and paradichlorbenzene. Mike walked by the cases at slow march, reciting the Latin names aloud as he passed. "*Scolopacidae*," he intoned as he passed the sandpipers. *"Larinae, Sterninae, Strigidae, Trochilidae, Corvidae."* When he got to the *Picidae*, he saw that someone had been working on a

112

taxonomic problem. A couple of trays were pulled out of the cases. In them, laid out neatly as squads of infantry, dressed to the right and covered, were the elongated carcasses of pileated woodpeckers, their eye sockets bulging with cotton, their claws curled in as if on some invisible perch.

At the end of the corridor he passed an enormous jar, four feet high, containing the pickled body of a crocodile, coiled like an entrail, white from its long immersion in alcohol. Down a hallway, Dr. Oberman's door was open.

The room was long and narrow, ending in a round, windowed turret. Books and journals stacked helter-skelter lined one wall and spilled over onto the floor. Along the other wall was a cluttered workbench heaped with specimen jars, dissecting tools, forceps, collecting bags, half a dozen corncob pipes, a hot plate supporting a grime-encrusted coffeepot, a glass-encased balance, a beautiful brass-barreled Bausch and Lomb microscope, a couple of low-power dissecting scopes, three aquaria, a glass-front cage holding a timber rattlesnake, some porcelain trays full of pondweed. A reeking cage full of white mice sat on the floor under the workbench. A couple of collecting nets were stacked in a corner over a pair of hip boots. The room smelled of tobacco, mouse excrement, stale coffee, pond mud and formalin. For a moment Mike wished his brother Andy were there—he'd go crazy with so many things to smell.

At the far end of the room, in the turret, at a heaped shambles of a desk, Dr. Oberman banged at an old typewriter, hunt and peck but fast. Behind the desk his great moth-eaten German shepherd, Kaiser Wilhelm, perked up his ears. Oberman looked up from his machine. *"Wel-kommen,"* he said.

Oberman was a huge bearded man with forearms that might have belonged on Ajax and a bad leg from World War I. He used a cane around the museum and in town, but when he was in the field he often abandoned it, and he could move through the woods or around a pond in a kind of lurching, crabwise gait that covered ground at great speed. At the museum, Mike knew, Oberman was not popular. He was given to roaring at people. He could be loud and undignified and unkempt, rattling about in his old wreck of a yellow convertible and followed everywhere by his great scruffy dog. A cross-grained man, during the war years he had made no secret of his Germanness.

As a young immigrant, he had been wounded fighting in an American unit in World War I, but he delighted in calling his dog Kaiser Wilhelm in front of people, and spouting the expletives that Nazi soldiers were always using in war movies and comic books. Mike adored him.

Oberman picked up his cane, swept a stack of scientific journals onto the floor from a chair beside the desk. "Come in, come in, sit down," he said. "You brought me something, *ja*? What is it?"

Mike sat on the chair. "Yes," he said. "Something pretty special, I think, that I got in the pond near our home. For the museum collection, if you want it."

"Let's have a look." Oberman took the bag, pulled out the jar. He looked at it, swiveled around in his chair so the sun shone on it. "Be damned," he said.

"He's in 10 percent formalin," Mike said. "Alcohol costs so much. You might want to transfer him."

Oberman whistled. "I'll be damned," he said again. *"Siren intermedia."*

Mike felt a flush of warmth rising in him. *"Nettingi,* I thought," he said.

"No doubt about it, you can see the light spots on the venter. Western Indiana is their normal boundary—this is really an interesting case of range extension. I'd have to check, but I wouldn't be surprised if this were the first specimen of *intermedia* taken in Ohio. Certainly we'd like him. That just shows what thorough field work can do. Now, my young herp, you've got some data on him, I trust?" Mike nodded, fished some three-by-five file cards out of his pocket. Oberman examined them one at a time. "All here," he said. "Location, measurements, good. Very professional, Mike."

Mike glowed. Oberman picked up the jar again, peered at the salamander. It floated there like a small, vertical man. "Wouldn't eat, huh?"

"He did eat, actually," Mike said.

"Disease, you think?"

"Well," Mike said, "I, ah, injected him."

"Oh?" Oberman eyed him curiously. "Not like you," he said after a moment, "from what you've told me of that menagerie of yours, to preserve a specimen as rare as this fellow, when you could have kept him alive. You know, around here we pickle everything. That's part of museum work. I pickle things. There are some people around here, like old Baulkins, who'd pickle their grandmothers." He paused. "A little reverence for life isn't such a bad thing in a biologist, you know."

Mike flushed, feeling subtly rebuked. "I thought you'd like him," he said, "for the collection."

115

"Sure," Oberman said, and smiled, friendly again. "I really do appreciate him, Mike, he's a prize. In fact if we send in your data we might get you a little item in *Copeia.*"

Mike nodded. Oberman sat and waited, the interview apparently at an end. Mike had hoped that he'd be able to slide into it, that Oberman would ask him about the pond where he'd got the specimen, and he could bring the subject up that way. But now he'd have to tackle it directly. "There is a matter on which I would like to ask your advice," he blurted.

"Oh," Oberman said. He stared at Mike from behind his beard. "Okay, shoot."

Mike began at the beginning, describing the pond in detail, the things he'd collected there, the Moses Cleaveland trees, the richness of life. He explained about the bulldozer and the development plans. The words came from him smoothly; he heard them fall on the museum quiet, mingle with the soft scratching of the mice in their cages, the dry slither of the rattlesnake in his glass case. "So," he finished up, "I thought that maybe you could help me."

Oberman leaned forward, his massive forearms on the desk, and looked at him closely. "That's why you killed the siren and brought it in?"

"Yes." Mike flushed.

Oberman nodded. "Buttering me up a little?"

"I guess so."

"So," he said, "now how do you think I can help you?"

"I don't know. I thought you might know. There's a museum conservation fund to buy land—I remember seeing something about it on the museum bulletin board."

"Hah!" Oberman laughed. "The conservation fund?

Mike, there's been a war on, that bulletin you saw is probably five years old. This museum doesn't have a pit to hiss in—I can't even get together enough money to mount a proper expedition."

"Maybe I could borrow the money," Mike said hesitantly.

"You could borrow . . . you are what, fourteen years old? Where are you going to borrow money?"

Mike stared at him. "Oh," Oberman said. "Oh, *mein Gott!*" He roared. "This boy is looking at me! At the pauper of the western world!"

After a moment he went on, his voice quieter, a little hoarse. "I am fifty-one years old. I make five thousand dollars a year, enough to keep my old car in gas, and I get some tobacco once in a while and my dog gets some meat once in a while. I have chosen as my own the poverty-stricken road of the dedicated scientist—oh, bullshit I have, but that's the way it's worked out. This mausoleum I work for, this sarcophagus, this crypt, has not coughed up a nickel raise for me in five long years. While every bohunk who can turn a screwdriver has been knocking down time and a half, I, a doctor of philosophy, a publisher of scientific papers, a man named Horst Oberman at a time we happen to be fighting the Krauts, I—I am the pickling pauper of the western world!" Oberman's huge hands gripped the desk top. After a moment he went on quietly. "I like you, Mike, you are a good boy. And you will grow up to be a good scientist. But I am not Mr. Chips. I can't help you."

"Yes," Mike said. "All right." He stood up.

"Mike, don't take it so hard. It is your pond, you love it because it is the place you are learning your science.

117

But there are other ponds. Things will be better for your generation. There will be money for expeditions. You'll be able to travel, to go to Africa, to South America, to go to Trinidad, like I used to, where there are bushmasters and fer-de-lances, and tropical nights and dark rum and beautiful women. It's all ahead of you."

"I understand," Mike said.

Oberman sighed. "No, I do not think you do," he said.

Mike turned then, walked down the narrow room. Oberman's voice came after him. "Mike." The boy stopped and looked back. Oberman smiled gently. "We'll go collecting sometime soon," he said. "With this leg of mine, I could use you to help me."

On his father's bowling night Mike sat in the living room stalking the Kumaon maneaters with James Corbett. Andy sprawled on the floor in front of the old claw-footed Magnavox listening to Jack, Doc, and Reggie in the "Adventure of the Vampire Bat." Andy was lying on his back, managing to eat fudge ripple at the same time by derricking spoonfuls of it to a point directly over his open mouth, then dumping them in with middling accuracy. His mother sat in her easy chair, crocheting. Her creation, once finished, dipped into a solution of sugar water and stretched over a form to dry, would stiffen in the shape of a vase. She usually made one or two of these every week to sell for pin money and, as she explained it, to keep her out of trouble. "The devil finds work for idle hands," she liked to say.

Mike had never been able to figure out what kind of work the devil might have in mind for his mother, as sin did not seem to be in her line. Certainly the devil would have a devil of a time finding her hands idle long enough to put any evil tasks into them. Her idea of self-indulgence was to move the small radio into the laundry room so that she could listen to "Stella Dallas" while wringing out the clothes.

Her skillful fingers moved quickly. Doc chattered with nasal excitement, while Reggie restrained him with British calm. Andy slurped fudge ripple. Mike read:

> As I approached the stream the tigress left the bush and came out on the projecting rock towards me. When I was within twenty feet of her I raised the gun and found to my horror that there was a gap of about three-eighths of an inch between the barrels and the breech-block. The gun had not burst when both barrels had been fired and would probably not burst now, but there was danger of being blinded by a blow-back. However, the risk would have to be taken . . .

Restless, he popped the book closed. "I'm going to put out some moth traps," he said.

"Hubba hubba," Andy said, trying to sound sarcastic.

Mike looked at his little brother for a moment. Then he said, "You want to come along with me?"

"Naw, I want to hear this program. And 'Gangbusters' comes on later."

120

His mother stopped crocheting. "That's past your bedtime, young man."

"Aw, jeez," Andy said.

"I don't like that language. Did you bring a napkin in here with that ice cream? Wipe your chin."

"It looks like the Black Hole of Calcutta," Mike said.

"Nerts to you." Andy sat up, wiped his mouth.

"That'll be about enough out of you, too," his mother said to Mike. "I went by your room today and I could *smell* it. I want you to redd up in there tomorrow."

"All right," Mike said, and got up from the chair. "I won't be late."

"See you're not," his mother said.

Mike got a flashlight and went to the front room of the hawk mews. There he kept a big covered crock in which he had brewed up a batch of moth "paint" a few days previously—a mixture of a couple of bottles of his father's beer, some molasses, and brown sugar. He removed the cover from the crock, blinked his eyes as the stench of the fermented mixture rolled against him. He ladled a couple of globs of it into an old paint can, picked up a brush from the shelf, and went out into the darkness.

He worked his way slowly up the hill through the woods, stopping every fifty feet or so to slap a brushload of the paint onto a tree trunk and making a mental note of its species and location so that he could find it again tomorrow. In the morning he would return early to check the traps. During the night moths and other nocturnal insects would have been attracted by the smell of the paint and would have fed on it until they reached such an advanced state of inebriation that they couldn't fly. Mike would pick out any specimens that interested him, particularly big handsome sphinx moths, and kill them deftly with a pinch of the thorax. The rest he would leave to sleep it off.

Without really intending to, he found himself drifting south to the area where the bulldozer had been working, and by the time he had emptied his can he was near the clearing. I might as well go see what it's been up to, he thought. When he reached the edge of the woods, he looked out over the slicked-down earth. The clearing had increased greatly since he had checked it last, stretching away toward the west, as far as he could see in the darkness. He didn't see the light patch of the dozer anywhere, and so he started across the clearing. Here and there he noticed fresh wooden pegs in the ground, marking out sites for roads and houses, and near the county road he found signs of work beginning on a new house.

As he moved on west, the quiet night ahead of him fractured into sound, a great whine and rattle, then a steady rumble as an engine caught and settled down. "Holy cow," Mike said aloud, "what's he doing running it at this time of night?"

Curious, he moved back over to the edge of the woods and walked slowly toward the sound of the machine. After a while he saw it dimly ahead of him, running without lights, and he slipped back into the trees a few yards and stopped to watch.

The dozer came closer, lurching from side to side. It stopped, went into reverse, and started backward with a roar, stopped, and came forward again. There was a clump of small locust trees at the woodline, and the dozer aimed itself and roared straight at them, then swerved suddenly almost at a right angle. It stopped and spun on its tracks like a whirligig beetle. Finally it got into reverse again, lurched backward, and ran straight into a big maple and stopped short. He's got to be drunk, Mike thought.

The dozer got aimed at the locusts again, charged them, and missed once more, this time churning by on the other side. Now it went around in a big circle and came rumbling down from across the field, inexorable as a tank. It hit the locust trees head on and rolled over them as if they were blades of grass. Then the machine stopped again, and he could see the figure of the driver, dim in the starlight, stand up in the driver's compartment. "Yippee!" the driver yelled over the engine roar. "Hi-yo, Pussycat! Ride 'em, cowboy!"

It was his father.

For another twenty minutes the bulldozer rolled erratically around the clearing, occasionally charging trees or brushpiles like a drunken elephant. Finally the man parked it near the edge of the woods, climbed down, patted it affectionately on its huge tracks, and then walked away across the field toward the county road, a little unsteady on his feet.

Mike waited until he heard, drifting across the field, the sound of the Cadillac's starter and its backfiring as it pulled away, and his eyes followed its pencil beams of headlights down the county road. Then he walked over to the dozer, climbed up over the tracks into the driver's seat and sat there astride the brute. He placed his hands on the steering clutches, looked out over the bow. "Varoom, varoom," he said.

From out there in the dark, he was answered by the high trill of a screech owl.

123

He climbed back down onto the track and moved along it until he could reach his hand into the darkness where the engine lay. He touched a wire, ripped it free. He felt around some more, found two more wires, and ripped them loose.

Going home through the woods, he flung them away into the night, one at a time, a hundred yards apart.

Dear Mr. Harrington:

In reference to your letter of July 7 to the Chairman of the Commission in regard to the Moses Cleaveland Trees on Old Oak Pond, pursuant to the articles of its charter, the Sesquicentennial Commission is authorized to identify and designate those trees in the Greater Cleveland area which are over 150 years old as Moses Cleaveland Trees. The Commission has no authority to purchase land for the purpose of protection of such trees or for any other purpose. Nor does the Commission have the authority to condemn land or to initiate legal action against landowners for any of the aforesaid purposes.

In reference to paragraph two of your letter, I am not precisely clear as to the meaning of your comments about the siren at Old Oak Pond. Under the articles of its charter, the function of the Commission is to arrange for appropriate ceremonies to commemorate the sesquicentennial anniversary of the City of Cleveland. If you feel that the noise from this siren is a disturbance to the neighborhood, may I suggest that you address your complaint to appropriate law-enforcement authorities.

Sincerely Yours,
Harvey Manors
ASSISTANT TO THE
EXECUTIVE SECRETARY

Dear Mr. Harrington:

Your letter to the chief in Columbus got sent up to me here for an answer, which is the way they do things. I'm sorry to hear about those old oaks, they sound like fine trees and there aren't many of those big white oaks left in the county. The Conservation Division does do some land acquisition. But to acquire land you have to get a line-item appropriation in the budget and get that through the legislature, and for the little parcel you're talking about, right at the edge of the city, you'd never get it, I'm sorry to say. And we can't just go around condemning land, although just between you and me, there are times I wish we could. The landowner can grant a scenic easement to the state or the county, but if he's already developing the land for a housing project you don't have a hope in H of getting him to do that. I wouldn't think so, anyway.

I've never seen a siren, but when I was a kid over in Ashtabula I used to catch some spotted salamanders at a pond there.

126

Sorry I can't be more help. Trees need all the friends they can get these days.

Sincerely,
Robert ("Bob") Fagerlund
DISTRICT FORESTER

One morning Mike put on his good pants, a white shirt, one of his father's ties, and his tweed sport coat. He combed his hair carefully in the mirror and took thirty cents from his money cache. He rode the streetcar to the end of the line, then walked six blocks, sweating in the tweed coat, along Bragg Road. The offices of E. U. Martincek, Builder and Contractor—like those of so many small businesses around Cleveland in postwar years—were in a modified quonset hut. The metal building was painted bright yellow, with small patches of grass in front, surrounded by a knee-high wooden fence, all very neat. Out back, some big earth-moving equipment was parked inside a chain-link fence.

Inside, the curved walls of the quonset were squared off with plywood paneling, the floor covered with linoleum tile. At a desk sat a young woman with blond hair and a tight black blouse. She was very pretty, Mike thought. He stared at her breasts. She looked up at him. "Yes?"

"I'm Mike Harrington," he said. The words came out almost in a whisper. "Mike Harrington," he repeated, louder this time.

"Yes?" the woman said again.

Mike felt hot in the thick jacket. *"Mike Harrington,"* he said loudly.

"I know that," the woman said. "Can I do something for you?"

"I have an appointment with Mr. Martincek."

"An appointment?" She stared at him for a moment. "Oh—oh, you're the one who wrote Mr. Martincek all those letters."

"I wrote him three letters," Mike said, "on a matter of mutual concern. And he finally wrote back and said to come see him on this matter of mutual concern at eleven o'clock today."

"That's right." She smiled suddenly. "Please sit down, Mr. Harrington. I'll see if Mr. Martincek is free." He sat down in a straight-backed chair. She stood up, came out from behind the desk. She was wearing high heels and nylon stockings, and Mike stared at the long sheen of her legs.

"You just make yourself at home," she said, and started through the door. She stopped and looked back. "Say," she said, "you sure can write a good letter. I went to secretarial school for a year, and I've worked here two years, and you wrote the first letter I've ever seen with a semicolon in it. I wouldn't know where to put a semicolon."

"It's easy," Mike said. "You use it to separate closely related independent clauses not connected by a conjunction, before a transitional connective, or to separate elements in a series when they contain internal punctuation."

"Well," she said, "I'll remember that. Now just wait a minute."

Mike sat there sweating in his coat and staring at the only item of decoration in the room, a calendar with a picture of a girl with huge breasts holding a crosscut saw. Under the picture was a caption that read, "Mister, I can cut you down to size," and in bigger type, "All your wood needs from Garrity Lumber Co."

128

In a few moments the girl was back again, standing before him on her long, beautiful legs. "Mr. Harrington, Mr. Martincek will see you now." Her voice was serious, but her eyes were smiling, as if she were enjoying herself hugely. Mike followed her down a narrow hallway between plywood partitions. She stopped at a door on the left, and before opening it, inexplicably, she gave his arm a squeeze and winked at him. Then she swung the door open and ushered him through. "Mr. Harrington," she said, the words coming out in a kind of bubble.

As he stood in the doorway, Mike confronted the top of a man's bald head. The man was working over a metal desk with a glass top, on which lay a clutter of paper, an ashtray overflowing with cigarette butts, and an enormous, chrome-plated wood screw. On the plywood wall behind him there was another calendar, like the one out front, showing another big-breasted girl leaning over precariously to deposit a log on a fire and a caption saying, "You bet I wood!" There was also a framed photograph of Jack Thompson, the high school football coach, autographed: "To Eddie, a loyal booster, Stub."

The man finished scratching at the papers on his desk and rose abruptly, stretching out his hand. His eyes came into focus on Mike. "What the hell is this?" he said. He looked at Mike. He looked at the girl. "What's going on?"

"Mr. Harrington to see you," the girl repeated, and went out through the door.

"What's going . . ." the man said. "That smartass broad . . ." His hand was still stuck out. Mike stepped forward and shook it. "Glad to meet you, Mr. Martincek," he said.

"I didn't expect a kid," the man said. "Well, sit down."

129

The man sat down again, looked at him levelly from gray eyes. "If you're looking for a summer job, we're full up. Besides you aren't old enough. How old are you?"

"Fourteen," Mike said.

"Well, you know you got to be sixteen to get a work permit."

"I'm not looking for a job," Mike said.

"Oh?" Martincek scrabbled through the papers on his desk, came up with several clipped together. "A matter of mutual concern," he read. "If you're not looking for a job, what did you write me all those letters for?"

"Sir," Mike began. Sweat was running down his back, but he felt calm. "I wanted to discuss a pond near your construction site located in District B–3, Map number 1723."

"What pond?" the man said.

"It's that one just off Elm Lane," Mike said.

"Pond?"

"The pond," Mike went on, "is known on the maps on file at the County Assessor's office as the Old Oak Pond. It is a lentic body of water covering three acres. Geologically, it is probably a kettle-hole pond, originated by the melting of a great iceberg sometime during . . ."

"What pond?"

". . . the Pleistocene."

"What pond?" Martincek's voice was rising. "What the hell are you talking about? What's this about the County Assessor's office?"

"The pond you're going to tear up for your housing project."

"You mean that stagnated puddle of piss up there off Elm Lane?"

130

"For three years I have been conducting a program of ecological research on Old Oak Pond," Mike went on. He wasn't sweating now; he felt totally cool. "According to my survey, Old Oak Pond is the habitat of nineteen species of amphibians and nine species of reptiles and a wide variety of aquatic insects. Last month I collected a species of *Siren intermedia nettingi,* which has never before been recorded in the state of Ohio."

"Siren what?"

"*Siren intermedia nettingi,* the western subspecies of the lesser siren salamander."

The man stared at him, but Mike kept going; he felt he was really rolling now. "Near the pond are three white oaks, *Quercus alba,* which are Moses Cleaveland trees, more than 150 years old, which I have registered with the Sesquicentennial Commission. I've also written to the State Division of Conservation about them."

"The State Division of what?"

"The State Division of Conservation," Mike said, "which is in charge of administering and protecting the state's natural resources."

Martincek looked pained. He scratched through the papers on the desk, came up with a pack of cigarettes, popped one in his mouth. He looked at Mike. "Ah, you want a cigarette?"

"A cigarette?" Mike paused. "Well, yes, I'd like one, thank you very much."

Martincek offered the pack, started to light his own, paused, reached across the desk, and gave Mike a light. Mike puffed, careful not to inhale. Martincek sat staring at him. They both puffed. "Okay," Martincek said. "Now what's this about your talking to the State?"

131

"Huh?" Mike said.

"I mean what are you trying to do, what's this with the State?"

"I registered the trees," Mike began.

"Don't give me trees," Martincek said. "Now what do you want? I mean, what the hell do you want?" The man seemed agitated.

"An easement," Mike said, calmly.

"A what?"

Mike took a drag on his cigarette, experimented with a French inhale, managed to accomplish it without coughing. "An easement. Under the provisions of Section 3, Article 55.4 of the zoning code . . ."

"Zoning code?" Martincek's voice was almost a shriek.

". . . it is possible for a landowner to provide a scenic easement for the state beautification program. Now, a little easement of about twenty acres would preserve the pond, the Moses Cleaveland trees, and a small sample of the habitat."

"Twenty acres?" Martincek said. He stared at Mike for a long moment. "Do you mean you want me to *give* twenty acres of that land to the State of Ohio?"

"You don't actually have to give it to them—you just promise not to build anything on it, that's all."

"I see," Martincek said. His neck was red above his collar. "I been working thirty years to build up this business, and now I get a break with the war ended and a real chance to do something if I can just hold all the pieces together, and now you think I'm going to take twenty acres of prime land and not build anything on it."

"I thought you might"—Mike took a deep breath before going on—"especially since there's another article of

132

the zoning code, Article 55.7, that says in District B–3 no dwelling shall be constructed within twenty-five feet of a property line, and if I understand your markers up there, two houses anyway are going to be closer than that."

Martincek glared at him. Above his collar the veins bulged. But when he spoke his voice was quiet. "And you are fourteen," he said. "Boy, you are some kid. I wouldn't want to meet you when you turn twenty. Now let me tell you something. I got a hundred forty-seven thousand dollars in debts, a prick-teaser secretary, a kid who got kicked off the Ohio State Football team, and a black-market lumber supply that's bleeding me white, and I can get along without you." He leaned forward across the desk, and spoke very softly. "You I don't need," he said. "I got lawyers who cost me a lot of money. I got friends on the zoning commission. Now, when you got your own lawyers and friends on the zoning commission, you just let me know, and then your lawyers can talk to my lawyers, and your friends can talk to my friends. Okay? Now get out of here."

"But I just wanted . . ."

"Get out of here!" Martincek stood up. Then, just as suddenly, he sat down again, and rubbed his forehead with his hands. "A fourteen-year-old kid," he said very quietly, as if to himself. "A fourteen-year-old kid."

Mike looked back as he went out the door. The man was sitting there holding his head in his hands.

Dr. Oberman called one day and asked if he'd like to go collecting. Oberman was doing some work on woodland salamanders and needed some specimens. Mike could help him roll rocks, he suggested.

The scientist came by the following morning in the old yellow Buick with Kaiser Wilhelm sitting on the seat beside him. Mike piled in, and they rolled off with the top down and the fenders flapping. "I need some red salamanders, *Pseudotriton*," Oberman said. "Do you know that one?"

"Yes."

"I've never found that many around here. We'll try out

at the county park. I think there's some question about whether we've got a real subspecies in this area. I want to compare them with some we have from farther west."

Within half an hour they were moving along one of the park trails into the woods. It was a mature beech-maple forest, dense with hemlocks in the ravines. It had rained the night before, and it was damp and cool and dark under the canopy of the trees. Here and there little red newts, glowing and orange as coals, sat along the path, driven from their homes in the leaf mould by the saturating rain. From high in the trees an ovenbird loosed its ringing cry across the forest.

Oberman cut off the trail and started down into a ravine. He swung along easily with his lurching gait, his cane over his shoulder, a corncob pipe stuck in his teeth, Kaiser Wilhelm at his heels. He stopped when he reached the trickling, yard-wide stream at the foot of the ravine. "This looks like as good a place as any. We'll go along the bottom here—you take this side and I'll take the other. Turn over any flat rocks, logs, big limbs, and pieces of bark, and be ready to grab if you see a red. Now remember, the underside of each one of these logs and stones is a mini-habitat, and biologists shouldn't destroy habitat. So let each rock roll back into its original position once you've checked it. You'll find lots of *Desmognathus* and *Eurycea*, but don't bother with them."

It was hard work, and muddy. Before very long Mike's trouser legs were sopping from kneeling on the moist woodland floor, and his boots were wet from standing in the little stream. But the discomforts were unimportant. He lifted stones, he pried under rocks, entering that small, secretive world of shy little creatures, so astonishing in the

135

richness and variety of its life. Centipedes and millipedes slipped away, their bodies undulating smoothly. Dusky salamanders, more slippery than fish, disappeared with a quick squiggle into the water.

In an hour he caught one of the little red salamanders, his hand on it quick as a cat's paw, and missed another that slithered out of his grasp. Across the stream, Oberman rooted around, prying things up with his cane. *"Schweinhund!"* he exploded once when his quarry got away. By the time they reached the bottom of the ravine where it leveled out onto the river flats, they had just two between them. They stopped to sit on an old log and rest while Oberman smoked his pipe.

"This is the life, hey, Mike?" he said. "Field work is good for the soul. Get out of the lab and into the world of living things. You know, I like my little vertebrates, but sometimes I wish I'd done mammalogy instead, so I could go off on behavior studies and live in the woods."

"I know," Mike said. "I like the lab, but I like this better."

"What's happened to that pond of yours?"

Mike told him about the visit to Martincek and about how the bulldozer was extending its range.

The scientist shook his head. "You can't stop it, Mike. This country has been in a state of arrested development for years. First the Depression, then the War. Meanwhile, we've been breeding like guppies till we're ready to burst our aquarium and spill out all over the floor. Look, do you know Malthusian theory—have you read about that?"

"No," Mike said.

Oberman prodded at the leaf mould with the point of

his cane. "You should read it," he said. "If you can read Darwin, you can handle this. Now watch." He drew a slanting line with the tip of his cane. "The available food supply increases like this, see, arithmetically—2,3,4,5,6, 7. But population—" he scratched a steeper line, diverging from the first—"increases geometrically—2,4,8,16, 32,64." He stabbed at the lines with his cane. "One day, if we go on like this, we will populate ourselves right into oblivion. That happens in wild animal populations all the time if the natural checks are removed, and it will happen to us. I won't be around to see it, and maybe you won't either. But you will be around to see the beginnings. In the next couple of decades, while you're growing up and I'm growing old, this country is going to change a lot. All this" —he waved his cane at the old climax forest around them—"all the places that you go and the places you want to go, they'll be finished, *kaput*. There will be instead factories and highways and houses and people. The air will stink, the water will stink, and whatever little land isn't covered with concrete will have a keep-out sign on it. And you"—he poked his pipestem at Mike's chest— "you, my brave young biologist, will not have any chance to stop it. Because all you are fighting for is the right to tramp around in the woods and catch some squirmy little creatures"—he jabbed the pipestem at the collecting bag that lay on the log between them—"some obscure little organisms that nobody knows about or cares about, and their rights to life and your rights to the life you want just aren't going to matter one infinitesimal damn."

Oberman paused, stared fiercely at him from behind his beard. "So," he said. "So—forget it. Forget your pond. There will still be some places to go—not here, but somewhere, where the heathen have been spared our civilization and our technology. Alaska for a while, and parts of Asia and Africa and South America—those are the places you must think about. Even they might not last your lifetime, but they'll last long enough for you to do some good science and to have some good times. There'll be those beautiful women, Mike, for you, on tropic nights when the smell of frangipani will drive you mad."

The man stopped abruptly. He drew on his pipe, then explosively guffawed. "Listen to Herr Doktor Oberman," he said. "The melancholy Kraut. The herpetologist Hamlet." He drove the point of his cane into the earth, levered himself to his feet. "Let's get back to work, Mike. For a field man, I spend too much time theorizing and not enough rolling rocks. Kaiser Wilhelm—*achtung*!"

They spent the rest of the morning working another ravine. Oberman caught one more red salamander, and then they had an encounter with a snake. As Mike moved along the gully, suddenly the snake was there a few feet in front of him, draped loosely along a moss-covered log. It was a pilot black snake, a big one at least five feet long, its body black and glistening and so immaculately fresh from a recent shedding that Mike could discern on its body a faint pattern of black on black, like charcoal on midnight.

The snake was frozen absolutely still but was quite aware of him. Its head raised slightly from the log, and now its quick tongue tasted the air.

Mike wanted to catch it. As Oberman stood watching, he approached the snake cautiously. He took out a handkerchief, dangled it from his left hand to attract the snake's attention. Then he leaned over, his right hand

138

poised. He waggled the handkerchief, then shot out his right hand to grab the snake behind the head.

He was too slow. The neck arced around, the lance head flashed, and he jerked his hand back. He was bleeding from two perforations in the web between his thumb and forefinger. Mike stared at his hand. The punctures were tiny, hardly more than needle pricks, but blood flowed profusely from the holes. "Nuts," he said, astonished. "He got me."

Oberman laughed. "You shouldn't take a big snake like that head on," he said. "Now, if you would like, I will demonstrate how a professional does it."

Mike watched, holding his bleeding right hand in his left. He expected Oberman to use his cane to pin the snake's head, but the man threw it aside, then crouched over the snake with his arms spread, looking like a Greco-Roman wrestler. "Now—observe." Oberman's hand flashed down and grabbed the snake not by the head but by the tail. "Ho!" Oberman roared, and whipped the snake clear off the ground and high into the air in front of him, then, in a fluid motion, whipped it back down and between his outstretched legs. As his legs snapped together, he pulled his hand forward again, stripping the snake through his thighs, and grasped its head with his other hand as it emerged from between his legs. He stood erect, holding the pilot's five-foot length between his outstretched hands. "So," he grinned through his beard. The entire maneuver had taken not more than two seconds.

"Jeez," Mike said.

Oberman laughed. "I'd suggest you not try that with a rattler," he said. Oberman brought his hands together, allowed the snake to loop its powerful curves over his forearms but kept a firm grip behind its head. "A magnificent specimen," he said. "It's odd that people should fear them so much, for they mean us no harm, and they are so graceful." He looked at Mike. "Do you want to keep him?"

"Yes," Mike said.

"All right then, but you have to keep him alive and healthy," Oberman said, his voice stern. "Keep his cage clean and very dry, and give him something he can hide under when he wants to. In a couple of days of seeing you around, he'll get used to you and become quite gentle—these aren't lunatics like the black racers—so you can handle him if you want to. He's very strong but not strong enough to hurt you. He's gripping hard now, trying to constrict because he's frightened, but when he settles down, he'll hold your arm just tightly enough so that he doesn't fall off. Wait for about a week before you try to feed him, and then give him a mouse or two each week, and that will be enough. You can even keep him over the winter if you want to."

"I can't bring him in the house," Mike said, "and the shed has no heat."

"Then you must release him in a proper habitat, like this, and before it gets too cold, so he'll have time to find a place to hibernate. Now help me get him into the collecting bag, and you can put your hand in the stream, the punctures should have bled clean by now."

They got one more *Pseudotriton*, and by then it was hot in the woods, and they were hungry and thirsty from their exertions. They returned to the car, and Oberman drove down the highway till they found a crossroads saloon. The woman behind the bar eyed them up and down, looked at their muddy boots and trousers, but took their orders for three hamburgers and a beer for Oberman and a coke for Mike. The woman had red hair and seemed old, as old as Mike's mother, but she had wonderful big breasts, he saw. Drawing the beer, she pressed the handle of the tap against them. Oberman, he noticed, was looking at them too. He wondered if he should ask Oberman about the secret vice. It would be too embarrassing, he thought.

Oberman quaffed his beer, licked foam from his beard. "Ahh." He sighed, and his eyes followed the red-haired woman as she went back to the kitchen. "So," he said. "So, you think you like the life of the biologist, Mike?"

"Yes."

"Ah, but I ought to warn you. It is not so easy, always. A life of penury, Mike, and the *Dummkopfs* will never understand—they will think you have bats in the belfry. In Germany, you know, we Krauts have such intellectual pretensions that all scientists have great prestige. But not here in the home of the brave. Some time you will meet some girl, and she will not want you because she thinks you sleep with animals or crawling things—and she knows damn well that you are poor."

He drank some more beer, looked around at Mike. "Still, there are compensations—like today. The field work is good, *ja*?"

The red-haired woman returned, bearing the hamburgers. As she placed them on the bar, Oberman said, "*Danke schoen.*"

The woman looked back at him suspiciously from her made-up eyes. "Are you German?"

"*Ja, Fraulein. Herr Doktor* Horst Oberman of Frankfurt and Berlin." She took a step back, and Oberman said in very precise English: "I was one of the designers of the V-2 rocket, actually."

The woman tossed her red hair, walked to the other end of the bar. Oberman watched her go. "Ah," he said, "sometimes it is too easy to get defensive, to erect the fences. We get too soon old—and we never get smart." He smiled then and said, "Come on, let's eat."

When they returned to the car, Oberman gave Kaiser Wilhelm the extra hamburger and said, "Well, we didn't do so well on the reds. Four will have to be enough."

Mike didn't want to go home—he wanted to prolong the day. "I know a place we might try," he said, "a couple of miles from my house. I collected there last year. It's a shallow ravine behind an old farm, and the habitat is just like where we were this morning, very wet, but the trees aren't so big."

"All right," Oberman said, "let's give it a try."

They drove back in toward the city with the top down, Kaiser Wilhelm between them on the seat. Mike leaned his head back on the seat and watched the tree branches whipping past against the blue sky. This is what life should be like all the time, he thought. This is the way I want my life to be.

They reached the county road about five miles west of the pond, and Mike directed Oberman along it. The old farm came into sight, and just beyond it the treeline came out to the road by the head of the ravine. "That's it there," Mike said. "You can just pull the car off along here."

Oberman parked, and they walked along the road shoulder toward the treeline. "What's that?" Mike said. A large signboard had been erected just back of the road

142

shoulder, but because they were approaching it from the side they could not read it until they got right in front of it. It was a sign made of a kind of fibreboard, professionally lettered, and it read:

PARKVIEW SHOPPING CENTER
18 stores to handle all your shopping needs
20 acres of parking
ARCHITECT: Thomas Benson
CONTRACTOR: James Ferguson Inc.
COMPLETION DATE: October 1947

Mike stared at the sign. After a long time Oberman said, "So, I'm sorry. But that is what I said. None of this will be left. They won't leave any of it."

"*Damn!*" Mike said.

"I know. I am resigned to it. But still, once in a while it does make you angry. I wonder . . ." Slowly the man lifted his cane, held it out ahead of him like a sword. He held it that way for a long moment, then, with all the power of his strong arm, he thrust it straight forward and drove its ferrule through the middle of the sign. "*Touché*," he said, and withdrew the cane. He turned to Mike, his face sober, and proferred the cane. "Would you care to join me in this token protest?" he said. "Useless, but good for the soul."

Mike took the cane, drew it back, and rammed it forward so hard that the impact jarred him to his shoulders. But he failed to penetrate the sign.

"Father always threw himself into our plays and romps
when we were small as if he were no older than ourselves," Kermit had written. "And with all that he had
seen and done and gone through, there was never any one
with so fresh and enthusiastic an attitude. His wonderful
versatility and his enormous power of concentration and
absorption were unequaled. He could turn from the con-
sideration of the most grave problems of state to romp
with us children as if there were not a worry·in the world.
Equally could he bury himself in an exhaustive treatise on
the *History of the Mongols* or in the *Hound of the Basker-*
villes."

"What a blue chip investment this is going to be,"

Mike's own father said from across the room. Mike looked up from the book, Kermit Roosevelt's *Happy Hunting-Grounds*. His father was sitting in his chair, a few pairs of Draft-eez at his feet. He was using the lapboard, figuring away on sheets of yellow paper. He lifted his slide rule, did a calculation, noted it down.

"I've noticed the world beating a path to our door," Mike's mother said.

His father looked up, grinned. "Come on, Martha, even a great invention takes a little time to put over."

The woman looked at Mike, nodded toward his father. "Lorenzo Jones," she said dryly, and pointed her crochet hook toward herself. "And his faithful wife, Belle."

"Oh, I know," the man said, "you're the long-suffering wife of the mad inventor. But you'll see. Marles is really interested in this, you know—he's nibbling."

"Maybe you could get him to just nibble up enough money to pay for all those samples you've been making, and then maybe we could pay some of the bills."

"I can't try to hurry him. If I seem overanxious, he'll just try to buy me out cheap, and it'll be just like that thermostat, we'll wind up with a few hundred dollars, and those guys will make the real money. Not this time, no ma'am."

The crochet hook moved briskly. "Just leave a few pairs of those things around," she said. "When the man comes to disconnect the phone, maybe he'll take some Draft-eez in trade."

"All right, Martha." There was annoyance in his voice now.

It was like that sometimes during late July, except that Mike's father wasn't around too much. Preoccupied with his Draft-eez, he took off after dinner in the Cadillac to meet with his toolmaker and prospective backers and returned late in moods that ranged from flushed and talkative optimism to a brooding, reticent depression. The thin metal strips, in slight variations of length, width, and thickness, littered the house like fallen metal leaves. Mike ran across them in the fruit cellar where he kept his collecting jars, on the mantelpiece in the living room, and late one night, going to the bathroom in the darkness, he felt something slick and cold under his bare feet and, reaching down, found a pair of Draft-eez there on the bathroom floor. His grandfather had always taken the newspaper to read while he was using the toilet; his father, apparently, had taken to pondering his Draft-eez.

His mother found him once, in the fruit cellar, looking at some Draft-eez his father had left on the shelf among the jars of raspberry jam and pickled cucumbers. "He's a dreamer," she said. "He always was. I remember when I met him. There he was with that secondhand Cadillac coupe and that ice-cream suit, you'd have thought he was John D. Gotrocks himself. And that head full of ideas." She had a jar of something or other in her hand, something she'd been bringing into the fruit cellar, but she seemed to have forgotten it. She said, "You're just like him. Another dreamer. You just dream about different things." She smiled and said, "It's all right, I guess. I'm just not much of a dreamer. Two dreamers to a family, that's all you're allowed." She turned then, quickly, and went out of the fruit cellar, leaving him there with the Draft-eez. She forgot to leave the jar she'd been carrying.

Mike spent the days working with Attila. Very slowly, and with frequent backsliding, the hawk began to "come

146

'round"—to accept him. He could look at the redtail directly without upsetting it now, and the bird no longer stared at him aggressively all the time. And it had come to accept, up to a point, the daily coming and going around the yard. But the sight of a feral cat prowling the nearby fields made the hawk grow tense and alert, and it simply would not tolerate the Harringtons' dog. One day the spaniel had the temerity to come bounding up while the hawk was worrying a piece of beef—the dog probably assumed that his ingratiating personality allowed him to share anybody's dinner. Totally unimpressed, the redtail fluffed its feathers out, came forward in a stiff-legged march, and lashed out with one big yellow foot. The dog yelped and bounded back, blood streaming from its muzzle. Thereafter the spaniel wouldn't get near the hawk if dragged on a leash.

Before he could hunt with the redtail, Mike had to train it. The hawk was already an expert hunter—otherwise it would not have survived in the wild. But to fly the bird at wild game before it accepted its human partner totally would be to chance that it would fly away and never come back. Thus, keeping it attached always to a long leash or creance, Mike taught the bird to fly to a lure made of rabbit skin and garnished with bits of meat, which he twirled on a cord above his head. Day by day, he increased the length of the creance until the hawk would fly to him without hesitation from a hundred feet away.

At that point, Mike began to cut back on the hawk's food, giving it only half a crop a day, trying to achieve that perfect balance between hunger and physical strength necessary before he could fly the bird at game. When the redtail reached a pitch of hungry alertness and Mike felt its talons grip through the glove whenever the hawk saw any movement—a grasshopper, a sparrow in the sky—it had reached the precise condition to be flown.

One morning Mike got up early and sat in the hawk mews and looked up at the bird. The redtail, aroused by the morning bird song, moved uneasily on the perch, looking out the window, which Mike had opened. The light streamed in on the redtail's golden brown feathers. Mike recited to it softly: "I caught this morning morning's minion, kingdom of daylight's dauphin, dapple-dawn-drawn falcon, in his riding of the rolling level underneath him steady air . . ."

"You smoking grapevines again?" Mike turned around and saw Andy there in the doorway, looking scruffy as he always did in the morning before his mother got hold of him. The laces of his tennis shoes were untied. He was eating a bowl of cornflakes. His nose wrinkled like a rabbit's.

"No," Mike said.

"What are you doing out here so early?"

"I'm going to hunt Attila."

"You're going to hunt Attila?" Andy's eyes widened in phony surprise. "What are you going to hunt? Elephants? Or maybe rats?"

"Okay," Mike laughed. "Tie your shoelaces before you fall on your face."

Andy came over and sat down, put his cornflakes on the floor, began fumbling with the knots. He sniffed some more. "You sure you're not smoking those grapevines?"

"No, smelly, I'm not smoking grapevines."

"It sure stinks in here," Andy said, "but I guess it's that bird. Are you really going hunting?"

"I'm going to try him on a rabbit."

"Hey, can I come along?"

"Not this time," Mike said. "You'd make him nervous."

"Some big brother you are," Andy said.

"This is serious stuff," Mike said. "Later on, when I've got him really trained, you can come along some time. Now wipe the milk off your chin."

"I'm going to work on the car with Dad," Andy said. He wiped his chin with his sleeve. "We're gonna put on a new head gasket. You don't even know what a head gasket is. You wouldn't know a head gasket from a distributor cap." He got up to leave.

"Take your bowl with you," Mike said. "How about keeping your cornflakes out of my mews."

"Yes, *sir*," Andy said. "No cornflakes in the *mews*. Hey, you might want to hunt around Karman's chicken coop—plenty of rats there."

"Get lost."

"I'll get lost," Andy said. "So will that buzzard of yours. First time you let him off his leash to chase a rabbit he's going to fly away and never come back."

"No, he won't," Mike said. He got up and moved toward Andy.

"Okay, Okay," the smaller boy said, backing out the door. "See you later."

Mike sat down again, stared at the bird, rubbed his hands on his blue jeans. The hawk was shifting nervously. "Easy, baby," Mike said softly. "You have to stay with me, huh, old Attila. You don't ever fly away from me, please." The hawk, listening, stared back at him through cryptic eyes.

"Here he comes now." Andy's voice drifted back from

outside the shed, high and nasal, in his imitation of Jack Graney announcing an Indians' game. "Here he comes, Mike Harrington and his famous rat-eating buzzard."

He walked slowly up through the field in the yellow early-morning light, cutting a thin, dark line through the glistening dew-wet grass, the legs of his jeans already heavy and wet from the moisture. The lure hung from his belt. Some pieces of beef, wrapped in waxed paper, were buttoned inside his shirt. The hawk rode heavily on his wrist, gripping its talons firmly into the leather glove. The bells on its legs tinkled softly on the quiet air as the bird shifted slightly. Song sparrows sang in the grass of the field. Chipping sparrows trilled along the edge. Occasionally, a songbird would fly across the field, and then Attila would watch it carefully, his talons digging into the glove. But he did not bate off after it—he seemed to know that such small, swift game was not for him.

Mike moved carefully along the edge of the trees. He had surprised bobwhite there sometimes but hoped he would spring none now. They were big enough to excite the hawk, but the whirring little birds were far too quick-winged, and it was important that the hawk not be frustrated. If he were disappointed enough, flown again and again but unable to catch anything, his confidence could be destroyed, and he could refuse to hunt at all.

Climbing the hill through the woods, there was a scurrying in the leaves off to the right, and the hawk roused, raising and ruffling its feathers.

"Oh, don't bate now, lovely," Mike whispered. "That is only a deer mouse, baby, nothing for you." Soothed by his voice, the bird settled on his fist again.

At the top of the hill they broke out into an open field,

and Mike felt the hawk's talons clamp down on the glove. He followed the bird's fierce stare, caught a movement in the grass ahead, and just in time recognized what was there, for the redtail went off his fist in a violent spring. "No!" Mike said. The hawk hung up at the end of its jesses, plunged downward head over tail. Out there in the grass, a big gray feral cat started moving back toward the woods, traveling quickly but not running.

The last thing Mike wanted was to have the redtail tackle a tough, old house cat gone wild and thus be exposed to injury. But the hawk had ideas of its own—it wanted that cat. It regained Mike's fist, immediately plunged off again. The cat disappeared, Mike hung onto the jesses, and Attila hung upside down from his fist, buffeting his legs with powerful wings. As Mike swung the bird back up onto his fist, it struck him in the face with its wing, bated off again. He felt blood filling his nose.

"Jesus," he said. He swung the hawk up again. It bated, thrashing its wings. Mike flinched. "Jesus," he gasped again, and the blood bubbled from his nose. "Easy." The hawk regained his fist, bated.

"God damn you!" Mike said. Blood ran down his chest. The hawk went off again, hung upside down, its beak open, hatred gleaming from its eyes. "Son of a bitch, hang there," Mike said. The words bubbled out of the blood running back down his throat.

Finally he got the hawk back on the glove. It sat there panting through its open beak. Slowly, ever so carefully, Mike reached around with his other hand and got a handkerchief from his back pocket.

"Easy, now," he said to the hawk, and put the handkerchief up to his nose.

The hawk bated.

151

"Oh, shit!" Mike said.

After twenty minutes the hawk had settled down, and he had stopped the flow of blood from his nose, though he could still taste it back in his throat, and it matted the hawk's scapulars. "How am I going to get that off you?" Mike said. "At least it didn't get on your primaries." He stroked the bird's breast. "It's not your fault," he said softly. "You're a brave one, to take on a cat. But I don't want you to get hurt. Now don't be discouraged, we'll get a rabbit."

They moved on down the edge of the clearing, the hawk quieted now, Mike watching carefully along the wood-line. Far back in the woods, a scarlet tanager called; from the tiny jewel-like bird came a sound like a taut rubber band being plucked, as if a frog were calling from the treetops. Mike moved slowly, slowly. He talked nonsense to the hawk. "Easy, baby, baby, easy now, such a lovely hawk, such a good old Attila, we'll both keep our eyes open now."

Nothing.

He worked back down the far side of the clearing, the sun a little higher, a little warmer. From the woods' edges, the bird song slacked off a bit with the growing brightness.

Nothing.

After another half hour, Mike feared that time was running out. If they found no rabbit soon, they would have vanished into their hides for the heat of the day, and he would have to give up, leaving the hawk angry and frustrated. He moved on purposefully along the woods' edges, working a little faster now, then crossed through some trees into another field beyond.

Again he felt the talons tighten on his fist, and in that

moment he too saw the rabbit. It was full grown, nibbling on grasses twenty yards out from the last trees. He froze. "There he is, baby," he said under his breath. The bird turned from the rabbit to look at Mike, eyes wide, questioning. Mike released the jesses. "Look," he breathed. The rabbit, still unconcerned, browsed on, the sun glinting golden on its fur, its antenna ears laid back.

The hawk opened its beak and stared at him stupidly.

"Oh, come on," Mike whispered.

The hawk clacked its beak shut. Then, inexplicably, it settled down on his fist, its talons relaxing their grip. Perhaps remembering its abortive attempt at the cat, the redtail had decided not to bother. "You can get him," Mike said under his breath. "Please, baby, please." The hawk stared only at him.

The rabbit made an error then. It started, made a bound, froze again in uncertainty. The beaked head swiveled, locked on target. The rabbit remained immobile, watching, its eye a still black bead. The hawk roused, its talons tightening like steel bands. Pain ran through Mike's hand, but he did not move.

The rabbit's ear twitched. The hawk turned its head and looked at Mike. "Please," he said. At the sound of his voice the rabbit suddenly burst away toward the woodline. "Go," the boy yelled. "Hoo-ha-ha!" He screamed the old falconers' cry, and he flung the hawk into the air. Twisting, flapping, the bird reorganized itself, somehow caught the rabbit's movement, cut toward it in a swirl of wings.

The rabbit was quick. It bounded diagonally back toward the woodline while the bird was getting up speed, disappeared into the grass at the edge of the trees. The hawk flapped about aimlessly, then lit on the branch of a dead oak at the edge of the clearing, closed its wings, and prepared to settle, beak gaping in frustration.

"Oh, no," Mike said. And the bird, at that moment, dropped out of the tree, did not so much fly off as flip into a slantwise dive, like an aerial bomb on its trajectory into the long grass. Its wings beating wildly among the seed heads, it disappeared behind the vegetation.

Mike ran forward, heart pounding. The hawk, there in the grass, turned toward him, beak agape and bloody, mantling, its wings half-spread to protect the warm thing that lay between its talons.

"Oh, you did it," Mike said. His voice was hoarse. He dropped to his knees. The bird hissed. Mike fumbled in his shirt for the packet of waxed paper. From it he took a strip of bloody beef, dropped it to the ground. The bird gulped at it, but kept one deadly foot vised onto the rabbit. "Here now, baby," Mike whispered, "let him go now." He dropped the next strip of beef farther away. The bird released its hold and moved toward the meat. "That's a good hawk," Mike said.

He picked up the rabbit by the ears and stared at it. A big buck, softly furred, almost unmarked except for drops of blood at its nostrils and mouth. "Oh, you are beautiful," Mike said. Then he got out his pocket knife and slipped the point into the animal's belly.

It took him half an hour to skin and gut the rabbit and build a fire and throw the badly hacked-at hindquarters on the coals. He gave the liver and kidneys to the hawk. Then he pulled a smoking leg from the fire and bit into it. Half-charred, half-bloody, the hair stuck to his teeth and the flesh burned his tongue, but he wrenched the hot meat from the bones of the kill and gulped it down, while the hawk, beside him, dipped its beak into the liver and lights. A little later, sated, Mike looked up to find the hawk staring at him, its beak crimson. For a while they looked at each other.

"I love you," Mike said.

During the long, locust days of August Mike worked on his collections. The big pilot black snake gentled quickly, just as Oberman had said it would. Hannibal, the fierce water tiger, simply disappeared. One day Mike went to the battery jar to feed it its daily ration of tadpoles and could not find it, even when he poked among the plants that grew up from the sandy bottom. Could it have crawled out, he wondered? He looked around on the table and on the floor, but he found no sign of the creature.

Each morning Mike flew his hawk. After the first couple of outings, the bird warmed to the hunt and seemed to rediscover its old, wild skill. Attila was a rather slow flier, but experienced, canny, powerful, and possessed of what Mike's falconry book called "a humour for killing." The redtail took a dozen rabbits, a black racer, and—in spite of Mike's efforts to prevent it—two feral cats, the mere sight of which seemed to fill the bird with ferocity. One day the hawk, coursing a rabbit, veered suddenly and dropped into some stubble. When Mike reached it, he saw to his astonishment that it was clutching a cock pheasant. It never could have caught the pheasant on the wing but must have spied it sitting close and simply dropped on it before the cock had a chance to explode into flight. Mike became so confident of the bird's growing steadiness that he longed to show it off to people. He took Toad with him twice and basked in Corcoran's admiration and envy. Once he even took his brother Andy—after making the smaller boy agree not to tell that they were eating the rabbits. "My God, Mom will think we've got tularemia and send us to the doctor."

Oberman called to ask him to go collecting again. Mike took the hawk along, hooding it and taking it with him on the streetcar to meet Oberman, enjoying the amazement of the conductor and the other passengers over the great bird that sat so quietly on his fist. Oberman grew enthusiastic about the hawk, and the collecting trip turned into a rabbit hunt, the bearded scientist lurching sidelong through the woods putting up game, and bellowing "Hoo-ha-ha!" when the hawk was flown, then crouching in a thicket to cook the kill. "We are savages at heart," he grinned, poking at the flames. "Beneath our civilized skins we are happy, innocent savages who want to hunt and eat red meat and scratch and fart and crouch by the fire." He wrenched off a haunch of rabbit. "That hawk," he said, and poked the leg into his beard. "*Gott!*" he said. "That's hot. That hawk," he began again, "is giving you something that few of us ever get, a door back, a door into your own primitive naked soul. Think about it, Mike." He wrenched off a piece of meat with his teeth, gulped it down. "A million years ago Java Man squatted by his fire and gorged on his bloody kill, and here you are, the same. What we feel now is what he felt. Welcome to the Dawn of Man."

The Dawn of Man—it did feel like that to Mike sometimes. Evenings, he would take Attila on his fist and go into the woods in the last hour before dark, not to hunt, but just to be there. He moved slowly and softly, trying to be soundless as air. He leaned against a tree and watched the dusk coming on, and his entire body felt sensitized.

He could watch for half an hour as the light slowly dulled on a single leaf, watch, as if his eyes were microscopes, the creeping progress of an aphid on a twig. Through his fist he could feel the fierce, pulsing vitality of the hawk, and there was a moment, one night, when he felt that he had become the hawk, entered its body and skull, that he was seeing with the hawk's telescope eyes; he could see, a mile away over the slope of the hill, the motes of swifts above the fields; he could see deep into the dark forest and pick out the slight motion of a squirrel in the treetops. His hearing stretched out and probed delicately through the woods, picking out and identifying each sound. He heard the dry rustle of a deer mouse in the leaves twenty yards away, the creaking wings of a mourning dove coming into roost in a distant hemlock. "I am Attila," he said to himself.

He saw Angeline sometimes, as he went up through

the fields past Karman's little house. Once, coming back through the woods with the hawk, he saw her out in the yard, sunning. She was wearing shorts and a halter and lying on a blanket on her belly. Mike maneuvered over along the woodline until he could see her clearly, then sat down in the leaves and watched. After a while she rolled over, lay on her back, and he could see her belly below the halter top and her lovely legs. "Isn't she beautiful?" he said to the hawk. The bird roused, looked toward the girl. Mike remembered the poem he had found in an old falconry book and said to the hawk:

> The falconer right makes well his flight,
> and maladies can cure,
> and then at night with sweet delight,
> can call his lass to lure.

"Don't I wish it," Mike said glumly. "I guess I'm not so good at calling lasses to lure, eh, old Attila?"

Down there in the yard Angeline sat up, began to rub suntan lotion on her outstretched legs. Mike watched her intently, continued to watch her for half an hour until she got up and went into the house. He went home then and tried to work on his moth collection, but he kept seeing Angeline's outstretched legs, glistening with suntan lotion, right there in the middle of the *Ios* and *Cecropias*. "Nuts," he said to the moths. "I am going to be a hermit and live in the Arctic and eat caribou and never see another woman." He spent the rest of the afternoon staring out the window.

He ran into her once, at Borden's Drugstore. She was sitting at one of the round tables in back, drinking a soda and reading a magazine. Mike ordered a chocolate Coke from Doc Borden, the bullet-headed druggist, who regarded the young people who made up his fountain trade with unconcealed malevolence. Mike stood at the marble-topped counter and sipped the Coke, glancing surreptitiously over his shoulder. Absorbed, Angeline didn't notice him. Finally, his courage screwed up, he walked on back, sauntering a little. "Hi, Angeline," he said very casually.

She looked up, startled, her dark eyes wide. "Hello." Her voice sounded a little scared.

"Can I sit down? I mean, there's no stools at the counter, and I hate to take up another whole table by myself."

"It's all right."

"What are you reading?"

She showed him the magazine. "They've just published Elizabeth's book in its entirety," she said. *"Nibbles and Me."*

"Oh." Mike looked down at the page. "Well, Elizabeth," he read, "we had a discussion about your chipmunk. As you know, animals *are not allowed* in the Commissary—but—in this particular case, I want you to know that we have decided to make an exception. We are *delighted* with the behavior of Nibbles." His eye dropped to the bottom of the page. "He is the cutest, sweetest, most adorable, and *adored* chipmunk in THE WHOLE WORLD."

"I think it's very sensitively written," Angeline said.

"Yes," Mike said, "it's quite sensitive."

They sat in silence then. Mike sipped his chocolate Coke slowly, trying to make it last. He looked around the store, then glanced up at the ceiling. A patch of it just above their table was festooned with the wrappers of soda straws, swaying in the breeze of the ceiling fan like the tentacles of an anemone. Mike knew the technique by which they had got up there—a kid would dip the end of the straw wrapper in the catsup from the hamburgers, aim it at the ceiling, and blow sharply up into the straw. The wrapper went up like a skyrocket and pasted itself to the ceiling. Was it, Mike wondered, a demonstration of Bernoulli's principle?

He looked back at Angeline as she bent over her soda, her dark hair hanging softly. Finally he said, "Well, I haven't seen much of you this summer, Angeline. I guess I've been pretty busy, training my hawk and everything. He hunts now. He hunts rabbit, and he's really good at it. He's, ah, unerring."

"That's nice," Angeline said.

"Maybe you'd like to go along one time," Mike said. "We go right up back of the house, not very far. It's really pretty exciting to watch him make a kill."

Angeline's pretty hands kneaded each other. "No," she said, "I better not do that, it would be muddy." She popped her mouth over her straw, began to suck up the soda as if she were in a hurry.

"Gee," Mike sighed. "I don't blame you, Angeline. The way I messed you up last time."

"That's all right," she said.

Just then Mike saw Marilyn Bishop come into the drugstore. Marilyn was wearing blue jeans and a halter top that stuck out in front dizzyingly. Marilyn saw them and came straight back toward them. When she reached their table, she stopped with her breasts at the level of Mike's eyes. "This crazy is after you again," she said to Angeline. "Remember what I told you."

"I was just leaving," Angeline said.

"What did you tell her?" Mike said.

Marilyn put her hands on her hips. "I told her you are some kind of nut, and she'd better stay clear of you. You've *got* to be a nut."

"I'm not a nut," Mike said.

"Anybody who jumps into swamps after some lizard is crazy," Marilyn said.

Mike looked at Angeline. "I'm *not* crazy," he said a little desperately. "I just collect things, that's all."

"You kill them and stick them in bottles," Marilyn said loudly. "I heard about you. You keep *snakes*. I read about somebody like you in the Sunday section who kept snakes and took young girls in the woods and *strangled* them."

"Oh, for crying out loud," Mike said. "Angeline, do you think I'm going to strangle you?"

"No, Mike," she said. Her lip was trembling.

"You better not try it while I'm around," Marilyn said. She glared at him. "Come on, Angeline, let's go. Let's get away from this goony loony." Angeline looked confused for a moment, but she rose, put her movie magazine back on the rack.

"Well, 'bye, Mike," she said, smiling weakly.

Marilyn smirked. "Good-bye, you jerk," she said.

Mike wanted to say something to her in return, something biting and witty, but he could think of nothing at all, and he sat mute as they walked away and disappeared out the door.

"I really," he said between gritted teeth, "I really, really." He put his face in his hands, kneaded his eyeballs. "I really, really, *really*—hate—stupid—people!"

162

"Hey!" Mike looked up. Doc Borden, the druggist, stood over him, bald head gleaming. "You do that?" Borden was looking straight down at him but pointing toward the ceiling. Mike glanced up at the straws. "No," he said wearily, "I haven't been doing that."

Borden's eyes narrowed. "I had that ceiling cleaned off yesterday," he said, "of all those goddamn straws you kids have been shooting up like you was all born in pigsties. It cost me ten bucks to get that ceiling cleaned, and now you're back at it already. Now those weren't up there an hour ago. You sure you haven't been blowing 'em up there?"

"You never can tell, can you?" Mike said suddenly.

"Huh?"

"A goony loony could do anything," Mike said. "A crazy, snake-keeping *nut* could do anything at all." He stood up, stuck his fingers in the corners of his mouth and pulled it awry, crossed his eyeballs. "Gorg, arg, blagh," he gargled at Borden. He jerked his fingers out of his mouth, thrust his hand toward the ceiling. "Mole the phantom strikes again!" he yelled, and then he ran out of the store.

During the last weeks of summer vacation he could feel his world getting smaller. An apartment building was going up on the big lot off Spring Road where he had once collected sixty-three garter snakes in a single morning, finding them coiled in half-dormant balls beneath the pieces of tarpaper he'd put out the previous fall. On Blair Road a block of new homes had already risen, and a line of new utility poles, wires humming, marched into the woods there. In the cornfields along the county road where he had hunted rabbits with the hawk just the week before, he found one morning a signboard announcing the construction of a new electronics factory: "Modern industry for a modern city."

One day, walking in the woods not far from the house, he found a red surveyor's tape tacked to a beech. He stood and stared at it. Oberman wasn't kidding, he thought. They really are going to take it all. By next summer there won't be any woods within two miles of here, and we'll be living right in the middle of the city.

A house had already been built in the honeysuckle glade, and a dozer had torn up the overgrown apple orchard where he used to go with his grandfather, the old man waiting beneath the trees while Mike climbed and shook the apples down, then paring off the skins in one long perfect spiral with his penknife sharp as a razor.

As he stood by the beech tree fingering the red tape, Mike closed his eyes for a moment and recreated the country inside his head. He could see in his mind's eye every acre of it, every square yard almost, every gully and thicket and woodline: where the coon tree was, the track the possums took down through the fields, the place to set a beetle trap, the sandy gully where the great hunter wasps filled their burrows with their paralyzed prey. Cardinals always nested in the brush near the mulberry tree. The best grapes grew at the place where the sumac trees thinned out, and you could make tea from the sumac berries; he had tried it once, and it was awful. There was a place far back in the second growth where half-wild peonies grew, with blossoms the size of your head; as a small boy he had fought them with wooden swords in summer, decapitating them with great blows, and had once brought his mother some on her birthday. There was an apple tree in the old orchard that his grandfather called a snow apple, the tiny apples bright red but white as snow inside, the best he'd ever tasted, and carpenter bees had worked busily at its old limbs. Orioles nested in the big

165

elm, hummingbirds in the young honey locusts, gold-finches in the buckthorn, hornets in the cedar on the hill. The milkweed burst in August when the butterflies came; the sap was white and sticky and good for warts, he'd been told. Half a mile along the Escarpment, there was a buck-eye tree sixty feet tall, with fanned-out leaves and branches spaced so evenly you could climb them like a ladder almost to the top. At the pond the night heron came just at dusk, crossing the darkening sky with its gut-teral, primeval squawk, to light on the border and freeze into immobility, the spear of its beak pointed down. Along the high ridge, after an early snowfall, he and his grandfather had found the tracks of a deer once—a doe, the old man had said.

In the spring the trees on the hill were a hundred subtle shades of green, a cool haze along the Escarpment. In summer, they were dark green and monochromatic; in fall, the maples blazed out like bright flames. In winter evenings, the air was blue as ice and tracks led every-where through the dark trees, and he would stand alone and absolutely still in the woods, moving his toes inside his boots to keep them from freezing, watching the dark fall, waiting for the snow to begin again, never wanting to go home, driven there finally only by the cold wind off the lake. He had seen a weasel once, white in its winter er-mine, come darting across the snow toward him in the dusk, hot on the tracks of some rabbit. He had started, and the animal saw him. It neither ran nor froze, but stood on its hind legs, paws in the air, bobbing and weaving like a boxer, darting its snake head toward him aggressively. A foot tall standing on its hind legs, it might have weighed half a pound, but it was filled with a mad belligerence and stood ready to fight him then and there. Suddenly the weasel dropped to all fours and darted at him. He stepped back quickly, and the weasel went straight across where his feet had been and off across the dusk-blue snow in long, fluid bounds, back on the trail of its prey.

Mike opened his eyes. He heard something coming, and looking around, he saw Mr. Karman swinging through the woods toward him, carrying a peck basket. The man stopped, nodded his beaked head. "Hello," Mike said.

Mr. Karman looked at Mike's hand, still holding the red tape. "Yesterday they come through. Three men. I saw." He looked up at Mike, smiled shyly. "Pretty soon no more woods," he said. "What you and me do then? Only you and me go in woods all the time." He held up his basket. "Today get pear. But not so many now, only two tree left. One more week, two more week, machine get them too. Pretty soon be just like old country, no woods left except for rich man." He shrugged, started down the hill. Mike followed along behind. They came out of the woods and crossed through Karman's neat little garden, where tomatoes hung heavy on their well-tended vines. When they approached the house, Karman stopped and looked at him. "My wife and Angeline go shopping," he said. "You want come in, have glass of wine?"

"Wine?" Mike said.

"Is okay. In old country even young boy drink some wine, little bit."

"All right," Mike said. "Sure."

They went on into the house, into a little back room where Karman kept his garden tools. The man put the

167

basket of pears on a bench there and took off his muddy boots, and then they went into the kitchen. Mike sat at the oilcloth-covered kitchen table while Karman got a couple of jelly glasses from the cupboard and a gallon jug of red wine without any label. "I make," Karman said as he poured it. "We always make at home." He sat down across from Mike, lifted the glass. "*E'ge'szegedre*," he said.

Mike sipped at the wine. It was sweet and pungent; he liked it. He looked around the little kitchen. It was very neat, with a plaster Jesus hanging on the wall, and it retained the spicy smell of Mrs. Karman's cooking.

"How is chicken hawk?" the man said.

"He's fine," Mike said. "I've trained him to hunt—he hunts rabbits."

The man nodded. "I know," he said. "One time in woods I watch. You not see me, though."

"Really?" Mike said. He drank some more of the wine. It was very good. "How are your chickens?"

"Still some go," the man said. "You right before. I find fox track. I set trap, but fox too smart. I never catch. Now I don't set trap. I don't care. Pretty soon no more fox anyway, no more chicken. You know zoning?"

"Zoning? Yes."

"Change," Karman said. "Next year, no can grow chicken."

"That's too bad," Mike said. He was feeling a little light-headed. "In fact, I'd say it's bloody preposterous."

"In old country," the man said, "can keep chicken, can keep garden, but no woods. Every place, just farm. If woods, then rich man own. If poor man take fish, take moshroom, get arrest. No good. I never like. So come

168

here, can keep chicken, can go in woods, have good job, have car. I like very much. So now can't keep chicken, machine eat woods."

"Thass right," Mike said. "Eatin' the woods. Eatin' my pond. Moses Cleaveland trees. Gobblin' it all up."

Karman refilled the glasses, and the two of them sat there in silence, sipping the wine. After a while Karman said, "You know my girl Angeline, I think she like you." He grinned from his wizened face.

"No," Mike said. "She thinks I'm crazy." He pondered that for a moment and then continued: "But she's ver' beautiful girl. Really beautiful, very pul—ver' pul-chritunuss." His words seemed a little blurry.

"She think you smart," Karman said.

"I'm reasn'y intelligent, I s'pose." Mike looked at the plaster Jesus. It seemed to be wandering around on the wall. "Just reasn'y intelligent. I don' like school, you know, Mr. Karman, it's so slow. I wanna go ta college. I'm goina Stanford or maybe Scripps Instituta Marine Biology."

"I think you do good in college," Karman said. He seemed to be smiling.

"Doarraight, I guess," Mike said. He sipped a bit more wine. "Education just a matter learnin' a-read. I can read three pages a minute easy."

"I come from old country, I go to school, learn English, too," Karman said. "Very hard. But I go. I learn. I can read newspaper, book. My wife, too."

"You know Theo're Roosevelt?"

"Roosevelt? Yes, I know. Good man. That Truman no good."

"He could read a book fast as he could turna pages."

169

"That very good."

"You know, Mr. Karman, you're arright." He stared across the table at the man. Mr. Karman appeared to be smiling. "Mr. Karman, I got a confesh to make. Never told anybody. You know secert vice?"

"I know," the man said. He looked toward the plaster ikon on the wall.

"I got it," Mike said. "Got it."

"Me, too," Karman said.

"You, too?"

"Sacred Christ," Karman said, and placed his hand on his heart. "I have."

"Well," Mike said. "Well, I don' have it all the time, juss little bit."

"Is all right," Karman said. "You just young boy."

"Huh," Mike said. "Sarright, huh? Well, that's wonnerful." Feeling pleasantly warm, Mike reached for his glass, saw that it was empty. He hoped that Karman would offer him some more wine, but the man smiled and put the bottle back up in the cupboard. "I guess we drink enough, huh?" he said.

"Sure," Mike said. "Enough." He got to his feet, focused his eyes on the plaster Jesus. "Well," he said. "Thank you ver'much." He got his eyes aimed at Karman. "I'm sorry about the chiguns. It's preposserous, I think." He started for the back door, then stopped and turned back toward Karman. "Say," he said, "you wanna go hunting with me an' the hawk some time? I mean, it's ver' inneresting."

"O.K.," Karman said. "Sometime we go."

"Fine," Mike said. "Swell. An' please con—convey my regards to Angeline."

170

He aimed himself toward the door and made it through and down the back steps. He got himself turned around and pointed toward home and started down the hill, feeling as if his head were floating in the air above him somewhere. It was a wonderful feeling. After a while he began to run.

It was just the next day, as he was checking his beetle traps up on the hill, that he became aware of a strange, distant sound coming from the direction of the pond. His head throbbed from the wine he had drunk, the day before, and he rubbed it gingerly now and said, "Well, at least you've found out what a hangover is." But when he stopped rubbing, the sound was still there, a kind of tocking sound, like wood being hit with a mallet. As Mike listened, it stopped, then began, stopped once more after a minute, started again. Mike fished a couple of beetles out of the sunken olive jar with his hemostat, popped them into the killing jar. The sound was there again. He started toward the pond to investigate.

As he grew closer, the noise grew louder. Crossing the fields north of the pond, something seemed strange to him, something was different about the appearance of the area. Suddenly he realized what it was—the skyline beyond the pond had changed.

Just beyond the pond he stopped and stared at the wreckage ahead of him. The westernmost of the Moses Cleaveland oaks was down, its massive trunk stretching away through the saplings that surrounded it, its topmost branches shattered like old bones from the force of its fall. Its severed trunk gleamed dully in the afternoon sun, strings of sap trickling down over the naked yellow wood.

171

A man in a hard hat stood on top of the trunk. He was holding a double-bitted ax. The man raised the axe high over his head, brought it down smoothly. *Tock, tock, tock* went the axe; hand-sized chips flew, and then a branch fell away.

Mike walked over to the butt of the oak, stood there before the great disk. A crosscut saw lay against it, and a sledge and a couple of wedges. Mike took out his forceps, and using them as a pointer, he began to count the growth rings on the butt, one by one. A few inches in from the bark he pressed the point of the forceps into the wood. "This is when I was born," he said.

He counted on, ring by ring. Some of the rings were wider than others, years of high rainfall when the tree had grown quickly. A foot and a half in was a space in which the rings were compressed—the old oak might have had a disease of some kind that had slowed its growth. Mike pressed the forceps into the wood again. "Abraham Lincoln was shot," he said. He counted a few more. "Civil War began." A couple of inches later, he stopped again. "Grant is a lieutenant, just learning how to use artillery in the Mexican War." The ax was still beating rhythmically, but he hardly heard it now. "The War of 1812, Perry is fighting the battle of Lake Erie." He stopped again. "Seventeen ninety-six, Moses Cleaveland founds the settlement at the mouth of the Cuyahoga River." The tree was already two feet thick then. He counted further and thought, Boone may have camped under it, slept under it with one eye open for the Shawnee. Or Simon Kenton before he ran the gauntlet. He counted a few more rings. "The Revolution," he said. "The bridge at Concord." The rings became harder to count then, in the heartwood, and he had to look closely.

"Hey!" Mike looked up. The man in the hard hat was standing over him, his axe in his hands, looking down from the trunk on which he stood. "What are you doing?"

"Do you know how old it was?" Mike said.

"What was?"

"The tree. It was way over 200 years old, maybe over 300. Here, where my pointer is, that's 1722. Hardly anybody but LaSalle had ever been out here. It was 60 years before the first white settlement in Ohio. There was nothing around here but wolves and Indians."

"What are you talking about?" the man said.

"The growth rings," Mike said. "I've been counting the growth rings to see how old it was."

"Well, it was a bitch to cut, I can tell you that," the logger said. "We busted a saw on it. And two more of these big bastards to go. I ought to charge double for this job. Now you better get on away from here. I don't like people around when I work, a branch might fall on you or something."

"No," Mike said.

"Huh?"

"I'm going to get my plaque." He walked around the end of the trunk, found the metal plate. "This is mine," he said. "I registered all three of these trees and got the plaques for them."

"Oh, yeah," the man said. "I noticed that."

"It commemorates Moses Cleaveland when he founded the city in 1796. I need a hammer or a screwdriver or something to get the plaque off," he said.

"Gee, I don't know whether you can take that," the man said. "I'd have to see what the owner would say."

"I don't care what the owner would say," Mike said. "These are mine, and I'm going to go home and get some tools and come back here tonight and take them off."

"Say, you are some tough guy, aren't you?" the man said. Mike didn't answer. "Oh, what the hell," the logger said. "It's no skin off my ass." He jumped down from the tree trunk, walked off through the woods to where he'd left his pickup truck on a track the bulldozer had cleared, came back with a big screwdriver. "Go ahead," he said. "Just don't tell anybody I let you do it." The man went back to chopping limbs.

Mike jammed the screwdriver in between the plaque and the wood, pried it loose, put it in his collecting bag. Then he went to the other trees, pried the plaques off them. He took the screwdriver back and left it on the seat of the pickup truck. Then he returned and sat on the stump of the old oak. The bulldozer had been working all around the stump, he could see from the tracks. It had dug earth away from the base of the tree and attacked the exposed roots with its blade.

Sometime later he heard a clanking noise and looked up to see the bulldozer bearing down out of the trees. It ran right up to the stump, the blade looming above his head, then stopped, backed and filled, reversed toward the stump. The operator cut the engine, climbed down, took his hat off, wiped sweat from the top of his head with his sleeve, looked up at Mike, grinned. "Hi, there," he said. "Better get down from there, kid, I'm going to pull this stump."

Mike stared at him.

"Come on down, now," the man said, his voice more impatient.

"No."

The man looked surprised. He stared at Mike for a

moment and then he said, "Say, aren't you that kid who talks about the weather?"

"Everybody talks about the weather," Mike said.

"Well, come on and get down from there."

Mike said nothing. The logger walked over, joined the bulldozer operator. "This kid won't get down from the stump," the operator said, his voice incredulous.

The logger nodded. "This is some tough kid," he said.

The dozer man looked back and forth from Mike to the logger. "Is this some kind of joke you guys are pulling? I tell the kid to get down and he doesn't get down. I don't get it."

"I think he's a little funny," the logger said. "He was here counting the rings on the tree and talking about Moses."

The dozer man stared up. "Look, kid, I said get down, I mean get down. Now."

Mike said nothing. The dozer man said, "What's the matter, are you crazy?"

"Yes," Mike said.

The man looked at him for a moment more, shrugged his big shoulders. "Okay, sit there," he said. "I'm gonna pull this stump whether you sit on it or not. Come on, Mel, help me rig the chains."

While Mike sat on the stump watching, the two men detached an enormous logging chain from the back of the bulldozer, wrapped it twice around the stump, looped it through some upthrust roots. When they finished, the dozer man came back to Mike, wiped sweat from his face with his sleeve, and said, "I tell you one thing, kid, you better hang on for a wild ride."

The logger joined him. "I don't think you'd better leave

him stay on there, Jack. If he gets hurt, we're going to be in trouble."

"I guess you're right," the dozer man said. "All right, kid, the game's over." He reached up, grabbed Mike's ankle and with one jerk flipped him off the stump, catching him with his other arm as he fell, setting him upright on his feet. "Now, young fella," he said, "you get on out of here."

Mike stepped back a few feet, stood there. The man glowered at him, then shrugged, climbed back up on his machine. The starter whined, the engine caught, and the dozer coughed and rumbled and roared into life. The man engaged the clutch, and the dozer clanked slowly ahead until the chain grew taut. The dozer lurched. The chain vibrated like a taut rubber band. The metal tracks bit into the dark earth, gouging it up. The stump did not move. The operator shot a look at Mike. Then he backed up his machine, maneuvered for a better purchase, roared ahead again. The stump didn't move. He backed off again, looked around at the stump, surveyed the ground, looked at Mike. "You think she won't move it?" he yelled down. "You'll see."

This time he backed the dozer all the way up to the stump. Then he revved his engine and let the brute go. The chain flipped off the ground, snapped taut, the dozer bucked and heaved, clots of dark earth spewed out from under its tracks, and suddenly the stump was moving, almost imperceptibly, rising and tilting like a gathering wave. The ground under Mike's feet was trembling, moving, and then the roots were coming, one thick as a man's waist rising from the ground beside him, slowly. He stepped back, and he could hear the roots snapping and tearing above the roar of the dozer, and now, quicker, the

176

great stump went up and over, and Mike stood staring into the gaping hole in the earth where it had been.

He did not get home that night until late. A light was burning in the kitchen, and when he went in, he saw his father sitting at the kitchen table with a bottle of beer in his hand and the single-shot .22 rifle across his knees. Mike suspected he was a little drunk.

The man glowered at him. "Where have you been, young man?" he said.

"Collecting," Mike said. He took his gas-mask bag from his shoulder, set it on the table.

"So you just didn't bother coming home for dinner?" the man said. "Your mother was worried about you."

"I'm sorry," Mike said. He went to the refrigerator, took some bread and milk. He felt his father's eyes on his back. "What's the gun for?" he asked.

"For that rat, that's what."

Mike turned from the refrigerator. "You mean you're going to shoot a rat with that .22? Here in the house?"

"Why not?" the man said. He shrugged, took another swig of beer. He must have had quite a bit, Mike thought. The old farmhouse did get rats from time to time, and his father hated them passionately, setting enormous, frightening traps baited with cheese down in the cellar. But he'd never got the .22 out before. Mike sat down at the table across from his father, began to eat his bread and milk. The man glared at him. The electric clock hummed.

"You kill things," the man said finally.

"What?"

"You kill things," he repeated. "Why shouldn't I kill things, too. I can shoot a rat if I want to."

Mike shrugged. "It's all right with me," he said.

177

"At least all I kill is rats," the man said. "You kill everything. That room of yours. Like a morgue, bottles of dead things all around you. The only things you keep alive are things that eat other things."

Mike's father went to the refrigerator, got another beer, put the rifle back on his lap when he sat down. "You been killing rabbits with that hawk," the man said accusingly, "and eating them."

"Oh, God," Mike said. "Andy can't ever shut up."

"I want you to stop that, you hear," the man said. "Your mother is afraid you'll get tularemia. You hear me?"

"Yes, Dad."

The man looked at him for a long time. "You won't stop it," he said. "You'll just keep right on doing it. I can't get through to you, can I?"

Mike said nothing. He finished his bread and milk, took the glass to the sink, rinsed it out.

"Where are you going?" his father said.

"To bed."

"Come back here and sit down," the man said. "I want to talk to you." Mike sat again. His father leaned across the table toward him. "Who in the Sam Hill do you think you are?" he said. "You don't talk to me. You don't talk to your mother. All you've done all summer is mope around that pond up there and go off in the woods with that hawk. You don't do anything with any other kids. You don't play any sports. You don't see any girls. I thought all this stuff was just a phase you were going through and you'd grow out of it. But you're not, you're just growing farther into it. You're turning into some kind of a—some kind of a specimen."

Mike sat in silence. His father sighed. "Thank God for

178

your little brother," he said. "At least your mother and I have somebody who talks to us. Do you think I'm stupid?" he asked.

"No," Mike said.

His father laughed. "Maybe I am stupid," he said. "I sure don't seem to be very smart." A pair of his Draft-eez were lying on the oilcloth, and he picked them up. He held them in one hand, bent them into a coil, let one end go, and the spring steel snapped back with a flip. "*Boing,*" he said. "Great for shooting spitballs. That's all they're good for. To hear anybody else tell it. You know," he said, "your father is a good inventor, he just can't convince anybody else of it." He put the Draft-eez down on the table; with six inches or so sticking over the edge, he held them down with one hand, plucked the loose ends with the other. They twanged gently. "*Boing, boinnng,*" he said. He shoved them away, picked up his bottle of beer, turned its bottom toward the ceiling, drained it. "I'll tell you something, Mike," he said, and put the bottle down. "It's a hard life."

The clock hummed. The refrigerator motor started up. "This is a great man-to-man talk we're having, isn't it?" his father said. "Quit sitting there looking at me like that. Go to bed, I don't care what you do."

As Mike started up the back stairs, his father called him. "Yes," he said.

"Stop by our room and tell your mother you're back," he said. "She's probably still awake worrying about you."

"Yes, Dad," Mike said.

It was much later, as he lay in his bed wide awake, that he heard the single shot, not loud, just a quick, sharp report. I'll bet he missed it, he thought.

He stayed away from the pond for three days, not wanting to watch the destruction of the remaining trees. When he finally did go, he didn't set out for there; he took the hawk hunting one morning, paid little attention to where the hunt was taking them, and as if some kind of magnet had been tugging at his feet, he found himself approaching the pond. The skyline beyond it had changed once again, a gap now where the second of the Moses Cleaveland oaks had stood. To the north, below the pond, he spotted a patch of yellow among the trees: the bulldozer named Pussycat, in a place where it had never been before. It seemed to him too early for the operator to be at work, but he approached cautiously just the same, moving from tree to tree until he could see the machine plainly, golden and dew-bright in the morning sun. "So that's what he's up to," Mike said to the redtail. The silent dozer had parked near the head of a gully, a dry watercourse leading down the hill toward Sandy Creek. It had started digging a ditch from the head of the gully toward the pond. "That's how he figures to drain it," Mike told the hawk. "The water will run down that old gully into the west branch of Sandy Creek." Mike stared at the ditch. "It won't take him long now, old Attila. He'll have that done before we know it."

A twig snapped. Mike looked up and saw the operator coming, walking down the track the dozer had made, carrying a bottle of water. The hawk roused. "Ssshh, baby," Mike said, and drew back a little farther into the trees, froze still. The man would pass close by him, but Mike was certain he'd never notice. "I wish you were a man-eating hawk," he murmured softly. As the man passed, the hawk's talons gripped nervously on the glove. "Ssshh." Mike stroked the bird's breast feathers gently.

The man clambered up onto his high seat, settled himself, fussed over the controls for a moment. The starter whined, the engine caught, and the hawk bated off Mike's fist. "Hey," he said. He got the hawk up again, said, "Take it easy." The hawk bated again, flapped wildly as it hung upside down. Mike looked back and saw the bulldozer was pointed in their direction. He got the hawk back on his fist again just as the dozer started down the track past them. The man was not going to work on the ditch now, apparently, and was taking his machine somewhere else. "Settle down," Mike told the hawk, "or he'll see us when he passes. What are you so nervous about?"

As the machine clanked past them, the bird bated off again and hung there flopping, then thrashed its wings as it tried to regain his fist. "Oh, nuts!" Mike said. But the dozer went right on by, the operator staring straight ahead.

Mike got the bird under control again, finally, though it still seemed nervous, rousing frequently, obviously upset by the bulldozer. Feeling glum, Mike crossed below the pond into what little remained of the fields beyond. "Maybe if we make a kill, we'll feel better," he said.

But they made no kill. The hawk seemed fretful; when they did put up a rabbit, the redtail missed it clumsily, then went up in a tree to sulk. Mike called it, whistled, proffered meat on the glove, finally got out the rabbit-skin lure and twirled it. It took half an hour of such coaxing before the hawk returned to the glove.

They moved on, approaching the other housing development off Blair Road. More utility poles had been put in, Mike noticed, and the linemen had strung more wire. In clearing a right-of-way for the utility line, a bulldozer had stacked up a lot of brush about thirty feet back from the poles, forming a line of heavy cover. "We might put something up there," Mike thought, and started walking slowly down the brushline.

It happened very quickly. Mike spotted a rabbit nibbling about thirty yards down the track, and Attila saw it simultaneously. Mike released the jesses, flung the bird into the air. The hawk, knowing that his quarry would break for cover, cut over to the brushline and stroked down it, fast and deadly. The rabbit froze until the last minute, but when it did break, it cut out toward

182

the stubble fields on the left. The hawk powered after it, low over the ground, twisting and turning with his darting prey. The redtail dropped once toward the grass but was up again instantly, screaming angrily. Having missed, the hawk curved back into a climb, apparently searching for a high observation perch.

"*No!*" Mike shouted.

The bird hit the utility line with the full power of its flight. The hawk did not scream, did not make a sound, but simply folded over the line, one wing on either side, and died hanging there.

Mike ran over, already knowing it was no use, and stood under the bird. Thirty feet above him it hung from the line like a snagged child's kite, its strong, beautiful wings draped gracefully down, moving lightly in the morning breeze. The nictitating membrane covered its eyes. The great yellow feet with the power of vises hung loose and relaxed.

For a long time Mike stayed there, sitting at the base of the utility pole and looking up at the hawk. When he left, the sun was high and hot.

He walked, then. He went west through the old farmlands till he came to the edge of the great earth plain where they were building the shopping center. He cut back across the woods of beech and maple to the construction site for the new electronics plant. Coming back through the hemlock grove, he found red tags on the trees there. Much later he returned to the pond, sat on the log and looked across the smooth, dark water. Off behind him somewhere, he could hear the sound of the dozer working. It was dark by the time he got home.

There was a light on in Corcoran's basement. Mike got down on all fours and looked in the window. Corcoran was there, fussing with his chemicals, peering into a test tube. Mike tapped on the window. Corcoran started, looked around the basement, went back to peering into the tube. Mike tapped again. Corcoran started again, this time looked straight at the window, puzzled. Mike pressed his face against the glass so Corcoran could see him. His friend made a wry face, started for the basement stairs. "You really spooked me, Mole," he said, when he opened the door. "I thought the poltergeists were attacking or something."

Mike followed him back down into the basement. "You're sure prowling around late," Corcoran said. "I'm glad you came, though. I'm practicing a chemical magic show I'm putting on for the Boy Scouts. You can be my audience." Corcoran got a folding chair, set it up eight feet in front of his chemistry bench. "Now sit there and observe the wonders. If you wish to show your appreciation, you may applaud at appropriate points."

Corcoran went back behind the bench. He rolled up his sleeves, picked up two beakers, each half full of clear liquid. "And now," he said. He poured one beaker into the other. "Presto chango," he said, and the liquid turned bright crimson. "And now the encore." He put a glass tube into the beaker, began to blow into it. After a few moments the liquid turned colorless again.

Corcoran grinned. "That's just a warm-up," he said. "Now some audience participation. Do you have a handkerchief?"

"I guess so," Mike said.

"Let's have it." Corcoran took it, flipped it open. "Slightly filthy," he said, "but for the purposes of experiment it will suffice." He stuffed it into two beakers of fluid, one after the other, soaked it thoroughly. He fished it out again, held it by one corner from a pair of tongs. "Observe," he said. He held the handkerchief over a Bunsen burner, and it went up in a sheet of yellow flame. Corcoran grinned triumphantly. "Mole cringes in horror as he sees his favorite handkerchief go up in flames, as he imagines his mother's implacable wrath on finding his snotrag a cinder." Corcoran waved the flaming handkerchief about. "But never fear, science to the rescue." The flames suddenly went out. Corcoran took the handkerchief by the corners, shook it out. "Not even singed," he said, "though still a trifle snotty." He grinned. "What do you think of that, Mole?"

"I want to blow up the bulldozer," Mike said.

Corcoran stared at him, still holding the handkerchief by the corners. "Huh?"

"The bulldozer that's tearing up the pond and everything. I want to blow it up. To smithereens."

Corcoran lowered the handkerchief. "Holy cow," he said.

"I want to make a bomb."

Corcoran looked at him curiously. "What happened?"

"I don't know. I'm just sick of it. The hawk got killed today. He flew into that new utility line on Blair Road. All the old snake fields and the ravine are gone for that shopping center. That guy on the dozer has been pulling up my Moses Cleaveland trees, and he's tearing up all the woods, and he's starting to drain the pond."

Corcoran shook his head. "You can't stop it, old Mole," he said.

"I can get even."

"Whew!" Corcoran said. He sat down on a high stool behind his bench, looked at his test tubes. He turned the Bunsen burner off. He looked back at Mike. "Say, why don't we go over and put some sugar in its gas tank?" he grinned.

"That's kid stuff," Mike said.

"Look, Mike, we've done a lot of fiendish things together, like making the Tesla coil last winter and jamming the radios all over town. But you know, we didn't get into really bad trouble when we got caught. People figure boys will be boys, and here we are, the brilliant young scientists, you know, and we got our wrists slapped and caught some hell, but people thought we were really clever, and we didn't get into real trouble. But blowing up a bulldozer—if we got caught at that, we'd go to *jail*."

"You don't have to do it," Mike said. "I'll do it myself. I just want you to tell me how to do it, that's all."

"Aw, Mike, this is really stupid."

"All right." Mike stood up. "I can read, I'll figure out how to do it." He started across the basement to the stairs.

"Hey!" Corcoran's voice came after him. He stopped and looked back. Corcoran looked very solemn. "Come down off the camel, Dickie," he said.

Mike shook his head and replied with Dick Heldar's words. "I want to be in the forefront of the battle."

They looked at each other for a moment. Corcoran sighed. "Come on back and sit down. You can't do it yourself. You don't know anything about chemicals, you'd probably blow yourself up." Corcoran sat down on his stool. "Let me think a minute." He stared at the bench in front of him, tapped away at it with a pair of forceps. He flicked a row of test tubes with his fingernail, making them ring. He fiddled with a pencil and a bit of paper. After a while he looked up. "It's not easy," he said. "There's glyceryl trinitrate—that's nitroglycerine. I think I could make it, I think I know how, and I could find out the rest, but it's just too dangerous. That stuff is so unstable, you need drowning tanks in case the reaction starts getting away from you. You remember that kid Reynolds, who won the city science contest last year? He tried to make nitro in his basement this summer and almost blew up the whole house. He probably let it get too hot. He lost an eye and an arm. So I'd just as soon not try that.

187

"Dynamite, same problem," he went on. "It's a lot more stable, but all it is is nitro mixed with some diatomaceous earth or wood pulp, so you have the same problem making it. TNT is stable, pretty safe, but I don't think I could make it. Nitrogen trichloride is explosive as hell, but you can set it off with a feather; we'd blow ourselves up just crossing the street."

Corcoran doodled on the paper. "Black powder," he said. "That's easy. But it's not very powerful. Maybe . . ." He doodled some more. "Maybe if I could give it enough compression." He fooled with his pencil and paper. "That might do it," he said. "We need a fuse. That's easy, I can do that." He looked up at Mike. "We'll need some chemicals. I've been helping Mr. Ray get the lab fixed up for the opening of school; I've been down there washing beakers and helping them take inventory, so I think I can swipe everything we need, except I don't know if there's any saltpeter there. I think that was one of the things he had to order. You better go to the drugstore tomorrow and buy a pound of saltpeter." He grinned suddenly. "If Doc Borden wants to know what you want it for, tell him you're going to Boy Scout camp and the scoutmaster asked you to get it to put in the milk."

"Thanks," Mike said. He got up to leave.

Corcoran came out from behind his bench. "I'm sorry about the hawk, old Mole." Mike nodded. Corcoran sighed. "I've got a feeling we shouldn't be doing this," he said. "But anything for science."

When he ordered the saltpeter the next day, Borden didn't ask him what it was for but looked at him curiously for a long moment. Mike didn't know whether it was because he was suspicious of the order or simply that Borden remembered him as the Phantom. But Borden said nothing and went into the back room. He was back there for what seemed like a long time. I hope he's not calling the cops, Mike thought.

He looked toward the back of the room. Angeline was there again with a couple of other girls—not Marilyn, fortunately. Watching her, Mike felt a rush of melancholy. She would never know of his secret passion, he thought. *"If I don't come back, Angeline," the Ronald Colman voice said, "I hope, once in a while, you will remember me."*

"Must you go?" the girl said, a catch in her voice.

"There are some things that a man must do. If I don't return, I suppose that you will marry Kermit one day. I would understand and wish you well. Good-bye—Angeline."

"Sixty cents." Mike looked around to see Borden plunk a small green sack on the counter.

Next afternoon he heard the resonant sound of the conch blowing. He found Corcoran at the old Basecamp, sitting under a tree. "Der egsperiment iss ready, *Herr Doktor*," Corcoran said. He got up, fished out of his pocket what appeared to be a ball of string. He held it up, waggled it. "Fuse, Mole," he said. "Created in the laboratories of Toad Hall. Now we begin the testing procedure. Step one." He got a carpenter's tape from his pocket, measured off precisely three feet of string. "Scalpel," he said. Mike fished out his Boy Scout knife. "Cut it right there." Corcoran tied the end of the string to a branch, draped the rest of it along the branch, studied it. "No," he said, "it will probably be hanging down and so burn a little faster." He let the string hang loose. "Now," he said, "we time it. Otherwise, we might blow our asses sky high tonight." He looked at his wristwatch. It was a new one with a sweep second hand. "You light it and I'll count."

"I don't have any more matches," Mike said, "they're back under the log."

"Some mad bomber you are," Corcoran said, dug some kitchen matches out of his pocket. "Press on."

Mike lit the string. It fizzled, puffed out some little sparks. Then it began to burn steadily upward, a glowing coal inching its way slowly up the string toward the branch.

"Twenty-three seconds," Corcoran said when it reached the branch. "A little fast. About seven seconds a foot. We'll want to use maybe five feet tonight, we want to be a long way off when this thing goes up. Now, step two. Scale model." He reached into his pocket, came out with a 20-gauge shotgun shell. The end had been plugged with wax, and a foot of fuse dangled from it. "The shotgun shell won't give the compression of course, but we'll get some idea. . . ." He hefted the shell in his hand, looked around. "This thing is going to make a heck of a noise, I hope nobody's around. What about that bull-dozer guy?"

Mike listened. The dozer was clanking off in the distance, down by the gully. "He'll never hear it as long as that machine is running."

Corcoran shrugged. "Okay, here goes." He flicked a match into flame with his thumbnail, lit the fuse, and threw the shell in a long arc into the trees. "Duck," he said. The two boys crouched down. "One, two," Corcoran said, counting seconds. "Three, four, five, six, seven —now."

There was an earsplitting crack and a puff of smoke over in the woods. Corcoran grinned, punched him in the shoulder. "What do you think of that?" he said. "That you don't learn from any Gilbert chemistry set. That, Mole, is *science*."

"But it was just like a firecracker," Mike said.

Corcoran shook his head. "Don't worry, Mike, that was the model. Wait till you see the real thing." Corcoran paused. "When do you want to do it?"

"Tonight," Mike said. He thought for a moment, and then said, "Why don't you just give me the bomb and let me do it. You don't need to come. It's a one-man job, really."

"Nuts," Corcoran said. "Now that I made this thing, I want to see how it works. Besides, now you've got me all stirred up."

Around five, Mike went into the woods to mark the point where the bulldozer would be left for the night. He found the man working at the ditch. Far enough off so he couldn't be seen, he sat with his back against a tree and watched through a screen of leaves. The yellow machine bucked back and forth, shoving dirt with its bright blade. It only had another few yards to go before the ditch was cut through to the pond. Instead of quitting at five, as he normally did, the operator kept on working, apparently deciding to open the ditch all the way, since he was so close. Around half-past five the dozer rammed up a wall of dark muck at the border of the pond, backed off, and stopped. In the silence, the man climbed down and stood over the ditch. Mike could not see into the ditch from where he was, but he could hear the water gurgling out. The man took his hat off, wiped his bald head, put his hat back on, stood with his hands on his hips looking down into the ditch. He nodded with approval. Then he got his water bottle and lunch bucket from the dozer and walked off through the woods toward his pickup. When he was gone, Mike walked over. He stood at the edge of the ditch. The tea-colored water was rushing out fast, carrying with it a swirl of life. Looking down he saw strands of elodea and little plaques of duckweed and tad-poles going past in a brown flood. He saw the silvery flicker of little bass, a sticklike water measurer, turning end around end like a log lost in a rapids. The ditch was a couple of feet deep; it would only begin to drain the pond. But the bulldozer would be back to deepen it, Mike knew. He stared at the big yellow machine. "Some bull-dozer will be back," he said aloud to the machine. "But not you."

As Corcoran had told him to, he scouted then, while it was still daylight, for an escape route to use after they lit the fuse. He found a faint path along the ditch and through the trees that he thought he could negotiate even in the darkness. There was a big down log back in the trees, and Mike, timing himself by counting, loped from the bulldozer to the log, not too fast, and jumped be-hind it. "One thousand twenty-three," he said. That should do it.

At dinner his father said: "You don't seem to have much to say tonight, young man."

"I guess not," Mike said.

"He's been moping around ever since his rat-eating buzzard got killed," Andy said.

Mike stared at his little brother. "Wipe the gravy off your chin," he said. Andy stuck out his tongue.

"All right, Andrew, that's enough," his father said. "That's too bad about the hawk getting killed, and you shouldn't make fun of it." His father looked back at him. "Well, school will be beginning in a few days, and you'll have things to take your mind off it."

"I suppose so," Mike said.

Andy said, "Mom, do we have any Fleischmann's Yeast?"

"Good heavens, no!" she said. "What do you want with Fleischmann's Yeast?"

"They always talk about it on 'I Love a Mystery.' They mash it up with a fork in tomato juice. I like the way it sounds when they do that."

"Well, we don't have any," his mother said.

Andy grinned. "It's supposed to be good for growing boys."

"Good Lord!" his father said. "I don't know where I got this family. A fourteen-year-old walking encyclopedia who won't talk to anybody and a ten-year-old human vacuum cleaner."

After dinner they sat out in the living room. His mother crocheted. His father sat at the side table fussing with his Draft-eez and looking morose. Andy listened to the old claw-footed radio, pestered to stay up late to hear the "Hermit's Cave," and finally won out. Mike went to his room about ten but didn't go to bed. He sat in the chair with the lights out, looking out the window. Lights were still on up the hill at Karman's.

"If I should die," he said aloud, "think only this of me: that there's some corner of a foreign field that is forever England." He wished that he could sound a little more like Ronald Colman. Again, as that afternoon, he was overcome by feelings of melancholy and loneliness. He thought of Kipling's poem about Roosevelt and said to the darkness, "Those who must journey henceforward alone have need of stout convoy now Great-Heart is gone."

He considered making a will. He would leave his equipment to Corcoran, of course, and his collections to Dr. Oberman at the museum. He would leave his air rifle to Andy, just to show him that his big brother was really all right. His diaries and scientific journals he would leave to Angeline, with a suitable inscription. Perhaps: "Though these may not mean much to you now, treasure them. They are my life's work. Perhaps someday you will understand. Michael."

The door opened, light from the hallway shafted in, and Andy walked through the door, a bowl of something or other in his hand. "What are you sitting there with all the lights off for?" he said.

"I'm just thinking," Mike said, and turned back to the window. "It's past your bedtime, isn't it?"

"I was just having a snack. I just came in to see you." He paused, still standing by the door. "I'm sorry about your hawk, Mike," he said. "I was just kidding before."

Mike looked around at him. "Thanks, little brother," he said. "It was nice of you to tell me that."

"Well," Andy said, "I guess I'll go to bed now. I'll see you tomorrow."

"Yes," Mike said. "I'll see you tomorrow."

When he went downstairs, the kitchen clock, illuminated by the faint moonlight coming through the window, said half-past two. He moved quietly over to the stove,

194

got a handful of kitchen matches, tucked them in his shirt pocket. It was very still. He could sense a faint scuttling in the floor under his feet. His father never had got that rat.

Outside it was chill. He shivered through his jacket. The half-moon gave plenty of light, and he went surely up past the mews, past the barn, through the fields. There was dew on the long grass and soon his trousers pressed cold and wet against his legs. When he entered the woods, the trees cut the moolight off, but he continued to move surely; he could have walked to the pond blindfolded if need be.

He felt as if all his senses were precisely tuned, in some state of super-awareness. He felt the subtle changes in temperature as the night air currents brought him through belts of slightly warmer, then slightly cooler air. He heard small scurries and scuffles as the deer mice went about their nocturnal wanderings. Far off, he heard the deep booming of a great horned owl. He approached the pond stealthily, softly as a Pawnee brave on a hunt. He could smell it. Then he could see the black water, glittering with the moon.

He maneuvered carefully until he reached the log. Corcoran wasn't there yet. He sat down and waited. Now that he had stopped moving, he felt the dampness even more; his legs were cold in the wet trousers. He shivered, hugged himself till the quaking stopped.

He watched the pond. Its level had dropped almost a foot since that afternoon, a rim of slime ringed the border now.

In the moonlight the water dimpled, then ringed out over the smooth black surface—one of the little bass rising. Down at the far end, he could hear the gurgling of the water as it ran into the ditch and down toward the gully.

Hunched there on the log, he felt a little light-headed. He imagined himself on a gallows, people arrayed below him, the noose around his neck. His parents, Andy, Corcoran, Angeline and Mr. Karman, Dr. Oberman, Martincek, all the kids from his class at school, Doc Borden. He knew exactly what he would say when the time came—he had found it in a book of poetry by Robinson Jeffers, to which he had been attracted by the title, and although the poem was tragic and difficult for him to understand, one line had stayed in his mind.

The hangman approached.

"You can skip the blindfold," Mike said.

"As you wish." the hangman answered, "Have you any last words?"

Mike looked over the assembled faces. His eyes were clear and dry, his chin firm, his voice steady as he said: "Give your heart to the hawks for a snack of meat, but not to men!"

He hoped they would· tie his legs, so they wouldn't twitch.

"There'll be trouble in the Balkans in the spring." Mike jumped. There was Corcoran's face in the moonlight, three feet away, grinning at him.

"You must have been having some hot thoughts," Corcoran whispered. "You must have been feeling up Angeline Karman."

Mike's heart stopped pounding. "Where is it?" he whispered.

Corcoran unzipped his jacket, reached in and pulled

out the bomb. He held it up so that the moonlight gleamed on its sinister length.

"*Holy cow!*" Mike whispered hoarsely.

The bomb was a big piece of iron pipe, eighteen inches long and an inch and a half in diameter, with the fuse cord wrapped round and round it.

"There she is," Corcoran said, obviously pleased with his work. "Big Bertha. Now that doesn't look like any firecracker, does it?"

"It sure doesn't," Mike said. Looking at the bomb, suddenly he felt frightened. He felt scared to even touch it.

"Have you got the dozer spotted?"

"It's over at the end there, by the ditch."

"How about an escape route?"

"I think it's all right. Twenty-three seconds, moving fast but not running, and a big log to hide behind."

"I hope it's real big," Corcoran said.

For a long moment the two of them sat there, neither of them speaking. Finally Corcoran said, "Scared?"

"Yes."

"I know," Corcoran said. "You want to call it off?"

"No."

"I don't either, now." Corcoran put out his hand, and when Mike took it, Corcoran gripped hard. "Intrepid Mole," he said.

"Brave Toad," said Mike.

Moving cautiously, Corcoran carrying the bomb, they went around the border of the pond. Mist was rising off the water now, ghostly in the moonlight. Their breath came in little frosty puffs. Mike, ahead, stopped abruptly, raised his hand. For a moment both were silent, then Corcoran whispered, "What is it?"

197

"I don't know," Mike said. "I thought I heard something. But I don't hear it now."

They moved on, all stealth now. Finally the bulldozer appeared between the trees, its yellow bulk glinting in the moonlight. "Jesus," Corcoran whispered, a catch in his voice, "it sure looks big sitting there."

They approached it, circled the gleaming blade, crouched beneath its tracks. Corcoran put the bomb on the ground. "Where's the escape route?"

"That way, down the ditch."

"Let's walk over it one time."

Mike led the way down the ditch and through the band of trees to the big fallen log. Corcoran looked around, tested the log by crouching behind it. "Should be okay," he said. "I'm glad for the moon, I wouldn't want to be stumbling around out there in the dark looking for this place when she goes off."

They returned to the dozer. "Now listen," Corcoran said. "When we get back to the log, you're going to want to stick your head up to watch her go. Don't do it. There's going to be a lot of stuff flying around out here." He picked up the bomb, unwrapped the fuse, handed it to Mike. "Your show," he said.

The pipe was icy cold in his hand. It seemed enormous. Mike stared up at the bulldozer looming over him, blocking the stars. He was trembling. "You all right?" Corcoran said after a moment.

"I don't know where to put it," Mike said, his voice shaky.

"I don't either," Corcoran said. "I couldn't find anything in the library about how to blow up a bulldozer, though there's a lot about how to get tanks with Molotov cocktails. Why don't you stick it up in front there, back of the radiator? The fan is up there, and the radiator and some other junk. It ought to do plenty of damage there."

"All right." Mike tried to place the bomb but couldn't reach far enough. "I'll have to climb up on the track," he said. He stuck the bomb in his belt, clambered up until he stood on top of the tracks. Breathing hard, he jammed the bomb into the machinery in front of the engine, draped the fuse down alongside the radiator. He climbed back down again, found the end of the fuse hanging at the level of his chest, got a kitchen match from his pocket.

He stood there. He could feel his heart pounding in his chest. His stomach seemed to have contracted into a little ball. He was breathing fast, but he didn't seem to be getting any air. He took three slow, deep breaths, then three more, and flicked the match on his thumbnail. It flamed brightly. He could see the end of the fuse hanging there in front of him, could see his illumined hand holding the match, could see the light flickering yellow on the mass of the machine above him.

"Light it!" Corcoran's whisper was urgent.

The match was almost down to his finger, Mike saw. He squared his shoulders. Then he said out loud, his voice steady: "Give your heart to the hawks!" And lit the fuse.

They ran. They did not walk in the quick, careful way that Mike had practiced that evening, but ran as if pursued by howling demons. Blinded by the flare of the match, not even thinking about looking through the rods instead of the cones, Mike barreled full speed into a tangle of blackberry bushes, felt the thorns rip at him. He pulled loose, the thorns tearing his face, then stumbled

199

into a tree. His breath came hard in panic. He charged off again in the direction of the ditch, almost fell over Corcoran who was picking himself up from the ground. "Jesus," Corcoran gasped, "where is it?"

"This way." He ran off down the ditch, Corcoran stumbling after him.

He stopped. *Where was the log? Over here, I think.* He ran to his left, then back to the right. *It must be almost time.*

"Here!" he heard Corcoran yell as he went shooting past. Suddenly, ahead of him, Mike saw the bulk of the log. He and Corcoran charged toward it and dove over the top. Mike landed flat on his belly, lay there with his face pressed into the moist earth, and the blood going pop, pop, pop in his ears. He gripped the earth with his fingers, trying to pull himself down into it and draw it around him, and waited for the great roar of the explosion.

Nothing happened.

He waited. He could hear his own labored breathing, and Corcoran's. A green frog twanged. The water from the pond gurgled softly as.it ran down the ditch.

He began to count. "One thousand one, one thousand two." Finally he reached thirty-five. Nothing happened.

Slowly, tentatively, he raised his head from the leaves, found himself looking straight into Corcoran's eyes, a few inches from his own. Corcoran said nothing but raised himself slowly, peered back over the top of the log toward the bulldozer. After a moment he said, "You sure you lit it?"

"I saw it sputter," Mike said.

"Nuts," Corcoran said. "All that for a dud. Probably the fuse went out, got wet from the dew, maybe."

Mike suddenly felt angry. "I'm going to go light it again," he said.

Corcoran shook his head. "If it burned down very much and you relight it, you won't have time for a get-away. I think we ought to sit here for a few minutes and make good and sure it's gone out, and the dampness hasn't just slowed it way down, then go get it, and go home."

"No," Mike said. "I'm going to relight it." He stood up, stepped over the log.

"I think you better wait a little while," Corcoran said.

But Mike was already walking back up toward the ditch. He could see now, his eyes had readjusted to the moonlight. He no longer tried to be stealthy; he strode straight toward the bulldozer. When he reached it, he looked up along the radiator for the fuse, but he couldn't see it. He climbed back up onto the track; he looked in front of the engine, but it was dark in there, he couldn't even see the bomb. He groped for the fuse. His hand found nothing. He peered into the darkness back of the radiator again. He saw it then, so faint his eyes could scarcely discern it: a tiny point of glowing red.

The flash was hot and searing white. He didn't hear a thing.

Dr. Vann came into focus slowly, materializing out of whiteness, as if emerging from a bowl of milk. He seemed flat, somehow.

He leaned closer. "Hello," he said.

"Hello," Mike said. It sounded funny, a mumble.

Vann shook his head, sighed. "Young man," he said, "you are very lucky to be among the living." Behind his voice there seemed to be a buzzing sound. "Do you remember what happened?"

"I remember a spark," Mike said. "Something glowing red in there."

"You were only partly conscious this morning. You

have been in the hospital for eight hours now. Fortunately, your friend Corcoran had the good sense to call an ambulance." Vann looked angry. Mike had not seen him since his brother Andy got into the hornet's nest and had to get shots, and he did not remember Vann ever looking that way before.

"Let me give you the inventory," Vann said. "Your eye is badly inflamed, but, thank God, nothing got into it. You'll have to wear that bandage for a few days and use some ointment I'll give you. This morning at six o'clock I removed about three dozen iron filings that your pal had mixed with his powder—from your arm. You have first and second degree burns from your wrist to your elbow. Your eardrum does not appear to be punctured. Can you hear all right?"

"There's a buzzing," Mike said.

Vann nodded. "I'll bet there is. We'll have to see, in a few days." His face came closer. "That you still have two eyes and two arms and two ears is a miracle," he said. "That bomb you kids concocted didn't burst, thank God, it just blew out one end of the pipe. If you'd been standing in front of it, it probably would have blown a hole right through you, but the blast just blew by you, and you got nicked by the edge of it."

He paused. "Kids," he said. "I deliver you, but I'm darned if I understand you. When we were kids, we raised some dickens maybe, but we weren't like you kids. Delinquency. Vandalism. Switchblade knives. Souping up cars and running them into phone poles. Drinking. Now bombs. I put the pieces back together when I can, but I sure don't understand it."

He stood up from the bed. "You've been under sedation and you'll be woozy for a while. I want you to stay here in the hospital tonight. You can go home tomorrow, but you'll have to come to my office every day to get the dressings changed on your arm. It'll be hurting you some. Just remember, you're lucky you've got an arm to hurt." He paused. "Your mother is outside. She's been here since five this morning. Your father too, most of the time. Sometimes, before you kids do the things you do, you ought to think about your parents a little."

She came in and sat on the side of the bed and looked at him. Her eyes were wide, red around the rims. Her hands were knotted on her purse handle. She unwound her fingers, put her hand on his bandaged arm. "You're all right?"

"I'm sort of sleepy," he said. "My ears buzz."

"We didn't even know what happened," she said. "We just got the call from the hospital, around 4:30, and when we got here the police were here, and your friend Corcoran."

"I'm sorry," he said. Her hand was twisting on the purse handle again. She looked very frightened. He wondered if she were frightened of him. "Where's Dad?" he said.

She looked down at the floor. Her eyes were moist. "He's been here," she said. "He went out a while ago, to see some people." She looked up at him. "He went to see if he could sell his patent," she said. "On the Draft-eez."

"What for?"

Her mouth twisted. "He—he wanted to see if he could get some money to buy some of that land up there. Your pond. So he could give it to you."

"He did that?" She didn't answer, just twisted her hand on her purse, and nodded.

"He didn't need to do that," Mike said. His voice sounded strange. "He didn't need to do that," he said again.

He was crying.

Up the hill, in the late afternoon sun, the trees showed the first traces of yellow and brown. Past the hawk mews, past the barn, Mike could see Mr. Karman moving the long, crude trestle tables out in the yard and Mrs. Karman covering them with white cloths. After a bit he turned from the window, moved slowly around his room looking at things, touching things, picking things up and putting them down, as if trying to find comfort in the familiar feel of his tools and his collections. His eyes touched his forceps and his hemostats, his collection of hunter wasps, meticulously pinned row on row like squadrons of sinister warplanes, the two luna moths drying on their spreading board, his egg collection with the perfect shapes nestled in cotton. He moved along the row of aquaria. The tadpoles had turned into small frogs now; the water boatmen and backswimmers spun and gyrated slowly in their tall battery jars, their poisoned beaks hidden against their bodies. As he passed the battery jar where Hannibal had lived, his eyes caught a movement. He leaned over to look more closely, and then he saw it. "*Oh,*" he said softly. There in the corner, a great adult water beetle hung from the surface, its elytra a rich chocolate brown and lustrous, the dusky plates of its thorax looking smooth and strong as steel. "So that's what happened." The water tiger during these last weeks had been buried in the sand, completing its magical transformation.

"Aren't you a bully fellow?" Mike whispered. "My ugly duckling has grown up."

205

There was a knock. He looked up and saw his father standing in the doorway. "Mind if I come in?" he asked.

"It's fine," Mike said.

His father stood in the middle of the room. "How's your arm feel?"

"It hurts a little. Not too bad. It kind of stings."

His father nodded. He put his hands in his pockets. "Well," he said. "I'm sorry I wasn't able to do it. In the end they just wouldn't buy it."

"I didn't want you to sell it anyway," Mike said. "You didn't need to do that."

The man shrugged. "Nobody seems to think they'll sell," he said. "Nobody thinks there's that much of a market."

"You can make them and sell them yourself now," Mike said, "like you'd planned."

"Yeah," the man said. He stood staring into the row of aquaria. "So I guess that's the end of your pond."

"It's all right," Mike said.

His father sat down on a chair, looked into the tank where the *Dytiscus* hung in the water. "We'll have to take you to juvenile court on Tuesday," he said. "Your friend from the museum, Dr. Oberman, he called when he read it in the paper. He said he'd come down to the court and talk to them. I talked to Ford, the principal. He's going to come down and get some statements from your teachers and Corcoran's. He thought with your school records and all, and being so young, you'd just get probation. I talked to Martincek. He seemed like a pretty nice guy. He was kind of—understanding. He told me about the time his kid got kicked off the football team. The bulldozer wasn't hurt except for some paint being scorched, so he

206

isn't bringing any charges. I don't think he really understood what you were trying to do. I think he thought it was just a big firecracker or something." The man looked around at him. "It's funny," he said. "You know, I've been designing pipe for twenty years. Pressures, stresses. I could have told you in two seconds that that contraption of yours wasn't going to work. But I guess you couldn't have told me what you were doing."

"I guess not," Mike said.

"I guess we can never tell each other much of anything," his father said. He stood up. He stood there with his hands in his pockets, looking down at the aquaria. "Old Karman is having his Labor Day picnic," he said. "All the Hunkies in town. We're invited. You, too. He said his daughter was worried about you being hurt. So if you want to come along, we're going up in half an hour or so."

"I look kind of funny. My hair and all."

"Well, suit yourself," his father said. He got up and started toward the door.

"Dad?" His father stopped, did not turn back.

"Yes," he said.

"I'm sorry," Mike said. "About your trying to sell the patent and, well, for making so much trouble for you."

"It's all right, son." His father turned now. "The thing that worries me is, I hope you're sorry you tried to blow up that bulldozer."

Mike looked down at the floor. The pattern of the linoleum was worn away, he saw. "I don't know."

His father stared at him for a long moment. Then he turned and went out of the room.

Later, Mike looked over his aquaria again, moving from one to the other. I guess I'll have to let them all go now, he thought. With the pond gone, he'd never be able to feed his collection. He leaned over the beautiful *Dytiscus;* it sculled about its tank, testing the power of its new legs. "Well," he said to it, "winter's coming anyway, so I guess it's time to let things go."

Restless, he continued to prowl his room. He read in his old journals for a while. He looked at the plates of elephant and zebra in *African Game Trails.* He went to look at himself in the mirror. A patch was taped over his eye; his hair was singed down to the scalp above his ear. His arm, fat with gauze, hung in a sling.

Eventually he went back to the window again, sat there looking out. After a while his mother and father came out of the house, his father carrying a hamper, and started up the hill toward Karman's, Andy and the dog tagging along after. It was coming on toward dusk now. The sun was gone from the treetops along the Escarpment. The swifts were out, arcing and curvetting in the sky above the fields, and some tree swallows, too, the first he'd seen since spring, flocking now for their flight south, coming down in little whirlwinds over the gooseberry bushes at the edge of the woods.

Up the hill, at Karman's, people were beginning to gather in the yard and at the long tables. Beyond them was the glow of a charcoal fire. He saw Angeline back there, near the fire, in her white bobby socks and a white sweater. A sound drifted down over the air, sweet and sentimental. Someone was playing an accordion, the "Blue Skirt Waltz."

He watched for a long time. "Well," he said at last. "Well, I guess I'll go on up there. I guess I might just as well."